She placed an arm around his waist. "Yes?"

"Have you enjoyed the evening so far?"

"Are you kidding? This has been the most fun I've had in a long time."

"It makes me happy to hear that."

"I'm happy that you're happy."

He stopped and turned to her. "Then only one question remains."

"What's that?"

"Should our next destination be the airport, to take you home and kiss you good-night at the door, or my place here in San Francisco, away from prying eyes?"

She leaned into him. "Mr. Drake, I want you to take me wherever you can fulfill your promise of leaving me fully satisfied."

They couldn't reach the Drake place fast enough.

"Wow." Aliyah stepped inside, immediately noticing the city view from their high perch in the hills. "This is beautiful."

Terrell came up behind her, kissing her temple as he wrapped her in his arms. "So is this."

She turned into him, desire in her eyes. The evidence of his desire was a little farther down.

"You know what I've been wanting to do all night?"

"Probably the same thing on my mind."

Dear Reader,

We've all met him at least once in our life. That guy. The one who thinks he has it all, an assumption only made worse by the fact that…it's true! He does! Success, swagger, fifty shades of sexy and any woman he wants. Such is the case with Terrell Drake, an unapologetic ladies' man who's always come out a winner in the dating game. Reminds me a lot of a guy I once dated. The one who was the one…well…until he wasn't. Like Terrell, this guy was 6'2" of mouthwatering hard candy with bedroom skills that could fill a college course curriculum.

However, unlike Terrell, he wasn't quite ready for a smart, ambitious woman who appreciated all he had to offer. Though not to the detriment of reaching her goals. He let a good one get away.

Suffice it to say, Terrell Drake has a different ending in mind.

Zuri Day

Silken Embrace

ZURI DAY

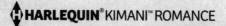

HARLEQUIN®KIMANI™ROMANCE

Recycling programs
for this product may
not exist in your area.

ISBN-13: 978-0-373-86429-4

Silken Embrace

Printed in U.S.A.

Zuri Day sneaked her first Harlequin romance at the age of twelve from her older sister's off-limits collection and was hooked from page one. Knights in shining armor and happily-ever-afters filled her teen years and spurred a lifelong love of reading. That she now creates these stories as a full-time, award-winning author is a dream come true! Splitting her time between the stunning Caribbean islands and Southern California, she's always busy writing her next novel. Zuri makes time to connect with readers and meet with book clubs. Contact her via Facebook (haveazuriday) or at zuri@zuriday.com.

Books by Zuri Day

Harlequin Kimani Romance

Diamond Dreams
Champagne Kisses
Platinum Promises
Solid Gold Seduction
Secret Silver Linings
Crystal Caress
Silken Embrace

Visit the Author Profile page at
Harlequin.com for more titles.

Sometimes the goal is worth the chase
Vying with many in the race
When you're heart to heart and face-to-face
Forever enjoying his silken embrace.

Chapter 1

"Good morning, Terrell." The attractive Drake Community Center employee's eyes sparkled with admiration and interest while traveling the length of his body.

Terrell Drake returned her greeting with a smile and a wink, aware of but unaffected by the blatant flirtation. He wasn't cocky. At least not more than the average Drake man. He was simply used to it; he'd affected the female species this way his entire life.

"Hey, Tee, what's up, man?"

"It's your world, Luther, I'm just trying to navigate it."

He bumped fists with the community center's executive director and kept it moving. Months ago when his mother had asked him to volunteer at the center as one of its assistant directors, he'd balked at what he thought would cramp his style. He'd been wrong. The joy that came from seeing a struggling student solve a math problem, or properly knot his tie, or curtailing a would-be bully's antics and have him see reason was beyond anything Terrell could have imagined. He actually looked forward to the three days a week he spent at the center. Walking into this after-school and summertime haven for more than a hundred children always made him feel good.

He reached the T-shaped end of the hallway and turned right toward the gymnasium. What he saw next made his heart skip a beat and wonder who owned the booty that, like sunshine, had just brightened up his world.

"Wow."

The owner of said gluteus maximus stopped, paused for a beat, then turned to look at him.

Wait, did I just say that out loud?

If he were to judge by her reaction and the look at her face? That would be a *yes*.

But that his slip caused her to turn was worth whatever was about to happen. The woman looked as good from the front as she did from the back. Better even. Her heart-shaped face was almost totally devoid of makeup, natural, the way Terrell preferred. She had big brown eyes, a pert nose and pleasingly plump lips to match her generous cleavage. All kinds of sexy oozing through that frown. Time to turn on the Drake charm. Terrell whipped out a smile that could sell toothpaste and closed the distance between them with a confident stroll.

"Good afternoon."

Her perfectly arched brow raised a notch. "According to whom?"

He had the decency to look sheepish. "Sorry about that."

"You should be." Her voice remained stern but he noticed a spark in her eyes.

He determined that he could get lost in those eyes. Holding out his hand, he said, "Terrell."

She paused just long enough to make him nervous, and then extended her hand. "Aliyah."

"Like the singer?"

Her scowl deepened as she shook her head and pulled back her hand. "No. Like myself."

"I meant no offense, was a real fan of her music." Terrell could deliver spot-on compliments in his sleep. Not today. From the look on her face, he'd just added insult to injury. He shifted his position to regroup and was just about to unleash his arsenal of amorous acclamations when he noted that Aliyah's weren't the only eyes watching him intently. He looked to her right, and down.

"Hello there, little man."

"Hi."

"What's your name?"

"Kyle."

Terrell held out his hand. "Nice to meet you, Kyle. I'm Mr. Drake."

The kid sized him up openly with a face that would do any poker player proud. "Are you my teacher?"

"I work with teenagers. How old are you?"

"Five."

"Five? Are you sure?"

He looked at Aliyah, who nodded. "He's big for his age."

"You might be raising a football player." She shrugged at his observation. "Are you here for the Progeny Project?"

"Is that what the mentorship program is called?"

"Yes, the Progeny Project."

She nodded. "We're here for that, and perhaps some of the activities the center offers. Kyle's young, but he's smart and easily bored. I'd like to get him enrolled in as many as are available to him."

"I can help with that. Follow me." He noticed that she hesitated. "Do you have another question?"

"I'm waiting to follow you."

She said it with just the hint of a smile. Terrell nodded his understanding. Any other brother would have assumed her hesitancy was because of what had happened moments earlier. Terrell knew the truth—time for her to check him out.

He placed a hand on Kyle's shoulder, encouraging the young boy to walk beside him. "Are you as smart as your mother says you are?"

Kyle nodded. "Yes."

"Confident, too," Terrell said with a laugh. "I like that."

They reached the end of the hallway. He led her to a set of double doors, and followed her into the general office area, where registrants were enrolled and files were kept. This area also housed three offices, including the one Terrell used when he was at the center.

"Hello, handsome!"

"Good afternoon, Miss Marva." Terrell walked around the counter and embraced the slight, older woman with graying hair tucked into a neat bun. The powder blue pantsuit she wore was topped off with pearl earrings and a matching necklace. Very classy. "Thank you for the compliment."

Marva laughed, entwining her arm with Terrell's as she looked into his eyes. "I'd say you're welcome if the compliment was meant for you. It wasn't." She looked at Kyle. "It was for this handsome young man standing by the pretty lady."

This statement won smiles from both Aliyah and her son.

"Whoa!" Terrell grabbed his heart. "You wound me!"

"You know what they say about assumptions. You brought that on yourself."

"I guess I did." He looked at Kyle. "She was talking to you, handsome young man."

Aliyah encouraged her son. "Say hello to Miss Marva, Kyle."

"Hello," he said shyly, before hiding his face behind his mother's skirt.

"Aliyah is here to enroll her son in Progeny, and to learn more about what our center offers."

"Wonderful! We'll get this young man signed right up."

"I will leave the two of you in Miss Marva's capable hands." He pulled out a card and presented it to Aliyah.

"If you have any other questions about the center or our programs, anything at all, please feel free to contact me."

She nodded curtly, then smiled as she returned her attention to Miss Marva.

Terrell reached the door and turned. "One more thing."

He watched her shoulders rise and fall before turning sideways to face him. "Yes?"

Their eyes met. The air sizzled, all but crackled between them. An unspoken, as yet unacknowledged attraction existed in each gaze.

"Never mind. Have a nice afternoon."

A little over an hour later, Terrell returned to the office. He walked behind Miss Marva, grabbed her by the shoulders and smushed her hair with his chin. "Get on away from me with that foolishness," she playfully chided, swatting blindly behind her while Terrell dodged and laughed. With a final squeeze, he let her go and walked to a set of file cabinets. Opening one, he began browsing through folders.

"May I help you, Mr. Drake? I know you think you own the world, but this office is my domain."

He retrieved a file, set it on top of the others and opened it. "You're absolutely right about that, Miss Marva. I'll soon be out of your way." Finding the desired document, he pulled out his phone. "I had to run earlier and just want to follow up on our latest registrant, Mr. Kyle—" a glance at the paperwork "—Robinson."

Miss Marva folded her arms, her mouth now as twisted as her lovely chignon. "And just what kind of follow-up do you think is needed?"

"The general kind, you know, answering any questions his mother may have regarding our program."

"Mmm-hmm. I've known you since you were crawling, Terrell Drake. And I am sure that the questions you want to ask that pretty lady have nothing to do with this center."

He tapped a button on his phone, placed the paper in the folder and placed the folder back in the file cabinet. "They absolutely do." He struck a professional pose—chin up, back straight. "And if those questions get asked over, say, a glass of wine or two, well—" he shrugged "—all the better, wouldn't you say?"

Marva's mouth untwisted into a lovely smile. "I'd say you're full of it and then I'd tell you to take her out and have a nice time. She seems like a sweet girl."

"Thank you, Miss Marva." After a quick look around, he lowered his voice. "And…let's keep this between us, okay?"

"I appreciate your stating the obvious, but this old trap has never sprung a leak."

Terrell went into his office, closed the door and tapped the number he'd entered into his phone.

"Hello?"

"Hello, Aliyah. It's Terrell, from the community center."

There was a pause. "Yes?"

"I had to rush out earlier and wanted to call and make sure everything regarding your son's enrollment went smoothly."

"Oh." Another pause. "Yes. The administrator, Miss Marva, handled everything just fine. Gave us a little tour and explained the program. We're all set."

"Good, that's real good."

A second ticked by. And then another.

"Is there…anything else?"

"Actually, Aliyah, there is. I'd like you to help me do something. Though it isn't very difficult, it doesn't happen often."

Suspicion coated the words she delivered. "Like what?"

"I'd like you to give me a second chance to make a first impression."

"That's really not necessary."

"I know. But I'd like to do it anyway—prove I'm not the cad my comment may have led you to believe. Something simple, say, dinner tonight. Casual. Jeans."

"I guess I can do that."

Terrell sat back with a satisfied smile.

"As long as regarding one thing we're perfectly clear. The part of my anatomy you found so intriguing will not be on the menu."

Chapter 2

Later that night Terrell was still thinking about Aliyah, surprised and a bit annoyed that she'd stayed on his mind. Sure, she was fine, but so were all the other women he'd dated. She was intriguing, but it was something more. An indefinable trait Terrell couldn't quite identify. He shrugged, focusing back on the computer screen and the news website he'd pulled up. It was just dinner. No big deal. That's why he'd suggested they meet at the Cove Café, the town's family-friendly diner, instead of the more upscale Acquired Taste or the always remarkable Paradise Cove country club. He didn't want to come off as trying to impress or anything. Why would he? Good looks aside, she was the parent of a student at the community center, with attitude to boot. Not mixing business with pleasure was Playboy Rulebook 101. With all of the women constantly trying to hook up with him, was a get-to-know-you dinner with her perfectly formed buns worth the messiness to his personal life that decision could potentially cause?

Yes.

Terrell ignored this answer that popped into his head, and the excitement that flowed through his other head as well. He wasn't in the market for a girlfriend and had enough friends with benefits to keep him more than satisfied.

So why was he taking Aliyah to dinner?

By the time he'd broken out his favorite pair of jeans, paired them with a navy button-down complemented by a platinum bracelet and thin chain, whipped out his solitaire diamond stud, removed his five-o'clock shadow and splashed on an exclusive blend of designer cologne, he'd convinced himself that he was just being a nice guy. That and he was hungry. Everyone had to eat, right?

He gathered his wallet and keys, and was heading to the door of his west wing suite when the estate's intercom sounded in his room.

"Terrell?"

"Yes, Mom?"

"Are you joining us for dinner, dear?"

"No. I'm heading out."

"Dinner meeting?"

He paused. "Something like that."

"Oh, I see. Have fun on your date, dear."

"Who said anything about a date?"

The sound of Jennifer's light chuckle made him smile. "Indirectly, you did. 'Bye now."

"'Bye, Mom. Love you."

"I love you more."

Aliyah pulled into the crowded parking lot, found a space and cut the engine. Grabbing a sweater from the backseat to ward off the slight October chill, she was pleasantly surprised to see the café Terrell had suggested was a homey-looking diner and not a swanky five-star restaurant. After getting Kyle enrolled in the community center's fall program she'd returned home, gone online and typed *Terrell Drake* in the search engine. What she'd seen there would impress most women. She was no exception. But it hadn't made her excited to meet him. She was all too familiar with men like him. Those who had the world by the tail, and thought they ruled it, from a family that practically owned the town or at least helped build it. One brother a grape grower and rancher and another one the mayor? Elite affiliations and country clubs for sure. The more she'd read, the more she'd been tempted to cancel their meeting. When he'd called and boldly requested dinner, and she accepted, it was to possibly secure a west coast casual who could periodically scratch her sexual itch. It had been months, she had been busy and a woman had needs. But now? With his lifestyle sounding so much like the ex whose family made it clear that she didn't and could never fit into their world? Why pull the scab off of a sore still healing? Because the attraction she'd felt in the community center office earlier was greater than her fear. So here she was.

She saw him right away, standing in a bar area with a group near the hostess stand. As she neared them he turned and reached for her, forcing the two women standing in front of her to step aside and let her through. Two men greeted her cordially and then walked away. The two women remained: appraising, waiting.

He made the introductions. Greetings were exchanged. He looked at Aliyah. "Shall we?"

"Yes."

"Ladies." With a nod goodbye in their direction, he placed a hand on the small of Aliyah's back as they followed the hostess to a corner booth.

But the ladies followed, hot on their heels.

"Did you have any trouble finding the place?"

Aliyah shook her head. "Not at all. Have GPS, will travel."

"That system does make it easier."

The woman closest to her, a cute brunette with expressive gray eyes, cleared her throat. "Where'd you drive from?"

Aliyah looked at Terrell, then turned to address the woman behind her. "Davis."

"You live there?" asked the woman who'd been fawning over Terrell when she walked in, and when introduced had offered a smile about as real as a three-dollar bill. The obvious competition, had Aliyah been in the hunt for a handsome, wealthy, well-built, charismatic, sexy example of male magnificence. She wasn't. So Nosy Nancy had nothing to worry about. And no need to know her business.

They reached the booth. Aliyah sat without answering. The server immediately came over. "Is this who you were waiting for, Terrell?"

"Yes, it is."

She placed menus in front of Aliyah and Terrell, then looked at the women. "Do y'all need menus?"

"Yes."

"No."

The server looked between Terrell and Nosy, from whom the simultaneous answer had come.

"It will just be Aliyah and myself tonight," Terrell said. "My friends were just leaving."

"Oh, okay." Expressive Eyes gave a general wave. "I guess I'll see you guys later." She walked over and joined the two men who'd left Terrell to sit at the bar.

"Speak for yourself," Nosy Nancy said, before looking at Terrell. "Are you going to scoot over or get up and let me in?" He didn't move, just looked at her. "This isn't a date, is it? I mean, you're at the Cove Café for goodness sake, so obviously—" she looked at Aliyah "—it's no big deal."

So this was how it went down in Terrell's hometown? Girlfriend didn't know but the poised, polite chick in front of her was east coast all day long, where people kept it real. She could switch it up and hurt her feelings. But instead, Aliyah ignored her. Why spar with someone trying to crash into where she had been invited? She casually picked up her menu and began to browse.

Terrell's voice remained low and casual, but his eyes

were those of someone who'd had enough. "You have a nice evening…okay?"

"Oh. Okay." She flung long black hair over her shoulder and adjusted a nice designer bag over store-bought boobs. "Sorry I upset you, Alicia. Terrell and I go way back, to preschool almost."

The misspoken name was intentional, and catty. Aliyah knew that, and offered advice instead of correction. "Don't be sorry."

Terrell's brief but knowing smile did things to her insides. The man was dangerous, too sexy for her own good. With no man in her life for the past few months, she wished he were on the menu she held. He had her so distracted she barely noticed Nosy mosey away.

"Sorry about that."

Aliyah's eyes turned devilish. "Don't be—"

"Stop it!" He laughed. "You know you're wrong. Clever, though."

"I learned from the best—been dealing with girls like her since I was fourteen."

"In Davis?"

"No. On Manhattan's Upper East Side, where I went to private school on a scholastic scholarship."

"You're from New York?"

She nodded. "Brooklyn, more specifically. Born and bred in Prospect Heights."

"But smart enough to go to school with the rich and privileged."

"Yes, and at times that was most unfortunate. I watched girls who had everything become jealous of one who had nothing."

He sat back, observing her keenly. "That's not true. You've got a lot."

"Yes, well, there's that."

"I'm not talking about your physical generosities…"

"Ha!"

"I'm talking about you."

"You don't even know me."

"But you make a brother want to know you. And that's what I'm talking about."

"Looks like you're a brother who knows everybody, and who everybody knows."

"It's one of the downsides of living in a small town. And one of the reasons I don't eat here often even though the town's dining options are limited. Everybody thinks they know you well enough to get all up in your business, even uninvited."

"Most women who act like that have a reason for doing so."

"She doesn't."

Aliyah shrugged. "Not my monkey, not my circus."

"Meaning?"

"Meaning whatever is between you two is not my concern. I just hope this place serves a good burger."

"It's not the best one in town but you won't be disappointed."

As if on cue, the server came over to take their orders.

Conversation halted as Aliyah perused the menu. Terrell watched. She noticed. "Clearly you've already decided what you want to order."

"Absolutely," he said, his eyes narrowing slightly. "I already know exactly what I want."

She rolled her eyes. He didn't know, but the action matched the roiling of her stomach as she took in the curly long lashes that framed chocolate-brown orbs, his cleanly shaven angular face and cushy lips. He smiled when she ordered the Cove Classic: double-patty cheeseburger, coleslaw and fries.

"Make that two," he told the server, letting her walk

away before he refocused his attention on Aliyah. "I love it. A woman with a healthy appetite and not afraid to show it."

She fixed him with a sultry look of her own. "Oh, yes. I have a very healthy appetite."

Check, and checkmate.

"So tell me about yourself, Aliyah Robinson."

"What would you like to know?"

"Since you live in Davis, how'd you learn about our center here in Paradise Cove?"

"A good friend recommended it. Her youngest son is enrolled there. She watches Kyle for me. So it works out."

"What's her name?"

"Lauren Hensley. Do you know her?"

"No. But I'm only there three days a week, tutoring and mentoring teenaged boys between thirteen and sixteen years old. A buddy of mine named Luther works with your son's age group."

"I wouldn't have pegged you as a guy who tutored teens."

"Why not?"

"I don't know. You just don't look the type."

"What type do I look like?"

Like the type of man I need to take home. Tonight. "Let me think about that." The honest answer remained unspoken, but a hint of it showed in her eyes.

"Is UC what brought you to Davis?" She nodded. "With all of the great schools on the east coast, why that school?"

"The residency program."

His brow rose in surprise. "You're a doctor?"

"Not for at least another two and half years. I'm in residency as an anesthesiologist."

"Impressive. Fine, smart…and you wonder why those girls were jealous."

"Things look much differently when you're fourteen."

"Indeed."

The server brought their drinks. Aliyah took a sip of her frothy root beer. Terrell had opted for real beer, and took a healthy swig from the bottle.

"Ever been to New York?"

"I've spent a little time there. My younger brother is going to NYU."

"What's he studying?"

"He's getting his doctorate in psychology."

"Oh, so you'll have a doctor in your family as well."

"We already do. My cousin's wife is a doctor in San Diego. But yes, Julian, hands down, is the brains in my family."

"Are you the brawn?"

He smiled. "Is that your answer for my type?"

"No, but if forced to fight I think you could hold your own."

"Ha! Thanks, I think. My family owns a realty and consulting company. I handle sales."

He was being humble. Due to her internet sleuthing, Aliyah knew he was a director in what appeared to be a very profitable company, heading up the sale of corporate and commercial properties throughout the state. A rich, successful, confident man who was also unassuming? Maybe he could scratch her itch after all.

"Is that how you ended up in Paradise Cove?"

"My grandfather settled here after leaving the military, went in with a partner and bought up a lot of land at a time when it was a buyer's market. After college, my dad correctly predicted that metropolitan expansion would push the population this way. So he acquired more land in this area, got his real estate license and partnered with a contractor to build homes. Thirty years ago, where we sit now was nothing but farmland. Now, we've got Paradise Cove and, next to it, Paradise Valley, where my brother Warren

now manages and co-owns that initial land my grandfather purchased."

"Not many people of color can claim such historical
ties and land ownership. You must be proud of what your
grandfather and father have done."

"I'm proud of my entire family."

Conversation continued. The flow was easy. The food
was good, the flirtations continuous. She told him a little
more about Kyle, and about the teacher/mentor-turned-
friend, Lauren, who'd encouraged Aliyah to choose UC
Davis for her residency. She also let him know that while
her body was in California, her heart still bled Brooklyn.
She was a New York Jets fan for life. Aliyah ascertained
that Terrell's extended family was a close-knit one, that
he was a member of the Raider Nation, but—that glaring
offense aside—there was substance behind the sexiness.
It was clear that neither wanted the night to end. But for
Aliyah, it had to. She had a son to pick up and an early
surgery to assist with in the morning.

She placed her napkin on the plate. "Thanks for dinner.
The food was delicious."

"What about the company?"

She shrugged, reached for her glass. "It was all right."

"Ha! Just all right, huh?"

"Yep." She finished the last of her soda. "Just all right."

"You're something else, you know that?"

"So I've been told a time or two."

"Well, hopefully I made a better first impression the
second time around."

She blessed him with a smile. "You did."

"Enough for you to go out with me again?"

She reached for her purse. "Maybe. But tonight's good
time has come to an end. I have to be up early in the morning."

Terrell reached into his wallet and tossed a couple bills

on the table. They stood and together walked out of the restaurant. He passed his shiny sports convertible and continued to her car.

"So, what kinds of things do you like to do?"

"I'm pretty adventurous and open to new things. There's probably not many things I wouldn't try at least once."

Her quick once-over suggested he was included in this statement.

"Is that so?" They reached her car. He opened the door. Before she could get in, he cut her off and pressed her against the metal. "What about Friday night?"

She didn't back down. She pressed back. "I have to work this Saturday. I'm off on Sunday, though."

"Then what about Saturday night?" He ran a strong, large hand down her arm, before resting it lightly on her hip.

"Highly likely, if I can arrange a sitter. But not here, in your town. I'm not up to watching you fend off women all night and if insulted again, I might not act as civilly as I did tonight." She pressed a hand against his shirt, and met a chest as solid as steel. "You work out."

"I do. As tight as your body is, looks like you do, too." Their bodies were close, their faces, too, so much so that their breaths mingled.

"Can't say much for crunches and treadmills—" she slid a finger down the side of his face "—but there are certain ways I like to exercise." She gently pushed him away and got into the car.

"Keep Saturday night open."

"Don't keep me waiting. Make a date."

"All right then. Saturday, seven o'clock. I'll text the details later."

"See you then."

She closed the door, started the engine and left the parking lot without looking back. Thoughts of Terrell accompanied her home, though.

Saturday night couldn't come soon enough.

Chapter 3

The days flew. By the time Saturday arrived Aliyah had almost changed her mind again about her date with Terrell. Though this was a woman's prerogative, she was usually more decisive. But he'd been on her mind more than was comfortable, took up more mental space than a potential casual should occupy. Trying to finish a three-year residency in two and a half was the only type of serious she could handle right now and something—okay, keen intuition and a heart that skipped a pitter when his face came to mind—told her that keeping things easy breezy and detached might not be possible. That scared her. So did the potency of her attraction. Yes, he was good-looking and yes, he was rich. She'd dated her share of handsome men and Kyle's father's family was part of the east coast's Black bourgeoisie. Her ex's family had doubted the truth of Kyle's paternity and shattered her self-esteem. She didn't want to go through that kind of scrutiny and judgment again, which is why a friend with benefits was all she wanted Terrell to be. But what if her heart felt otherwise? Did she want to chance a hot, sexual fling blazing into a relationship? Or worse, an inferno?

When she'd pulled up stakes and left the east coast, falling for an obvious heartthrob within a month of arriving hadn't been in her plans. It still wasn't. At least through this year, the only male she planned to focus on was the not yet three-foot-tall, sweet and curious tyke standing in front of her with his ever-present tablet in hand. But unlike most kids, Kyle was as likely to be working math problems from the study modules she'd downloaded as playing video games. The child had an unusual interest in numbers. She'd purchased the kid-friendly program to encourage him. Being good with numbers could take you places.

"Where are you going, Mommy?"

"Out with a friend, sweetheart."

"Is it Mr. Drake?"

Aliyah was stunned, but maintained her composure by putting on her earring before she turned around. "What makes you think Mr. Drake and I are friends?"

"Because."

Aliyah watched as her son held his arms out to the side and "flew" around the room. He could never sit still. She walked over to where he was and placed hands on his shoulders to still him. "Because what?"

"Because of how he was smiling when you came to pick us up."

On Friday Lauren's teenaged son, Conrad, had fractured his arm while skateboarding. On her way to emergency she'd called Aliyah, who agreed to pick up Kyle and Conner from the center.

"Mr. Drake wasn't there, honey, remember? I spoke with your teacher, Mr. Adams."

"I know, but Mr. Drake saw you, too. He stopped in the hallway and started smiling. Like this."

Kyle smiled broadly. Aliyah laughed.

Observant little bugger. *Note to self: watch your actions with Terrell when Kyle is around.*

"I think he wanted to say hi, but this woman came and got him."

A scowl jumped on her face without her permission, before she could stop it. The unconscious reaction surprised her. No doubt Terrell was popular with the ladies. And obviously unattached. Why wouldn't they be swarming around him like bees on a honeycomb? And why should it matter to her? All she wanted from him was some horizontal exercise. She vowed to remember that.

"Do you see Mr. Drake often?"

"Yes. He comes and talks to Mr. Adams. They're good friends."

"How do you know?"

"They laugh a lot."

"Oh."

Kyle sat on the bench at the foot of her bed, tapped the face of the tablet and restarted a numbers game. "I like Mr. Drake."

"Why?"

He shrugged. "Because he is cool."

Great. Even her son was smitten. Well, Mr. Cool made Mommy hot, and glad that Luther Adams was Kyle's main teacher. Not good for her son to get too attached to a man in their lives only temporarily. She walked over to the closet and stood in front of a row of shoes, deciding. She was in no way trying to impress Mr. Drake, but still bypassed the comfy flats and chose a pair of strappy crystal-covered stilettos to pair with her black skinny jeans and off-the-shoulder cream-colored top. "Go get your Power Ranger backpack. It's packed with clothes for you."

Kyle looked up. "Where am I going?"

"Oh. I didn't tell you? You've been invited to Conner's house for an overnight playdate."

"Awesome!"

She laughed as he ran from the room, his interest in Mommy's date, who just happened to be with Mr. Cool, totally forgotten. It had been Lauren's idea to have Kyle spend the night. They were good friends who shared almost everything. Lauren was probably just as excited that Aliyah might get some as she was.

A few minutes later and they were in the car and headed to the Hensleys, whose house was mere blocks away. She only had a few minutes once they arrived, but she still got out of the car to greet her mentor and best friend.

"Hey, girl."

"Hey yourself. Don't you look snazzy!" Leaning in, Lauren whispered, "I especially love those F-me pumps."

Rather than disagree, Aliyah cosigned. "If I'm lucky!"

They laughed and high-fived.

Aliyah had met Lauren during her sophomore year in high school. At that time, Lauren worked as a counselor at the academy Aliyah attended. A raven-haired, free-spirited thirtysomething cutie from California, Lauren quickly picked up on some of Aliyah's classmates' antics. She paid special attention to Aliyah, not only for that reason, but also because she was so smart. And driven, too. When Aliyah announced her plans to become a doctor, Lauren was her biggest cheerleader, helping Aliyah choose appropriate classes and complete scholarship applications. Once Aliyah graduated high school, the two kept in touch and when she got pregnant, it was Lauren that Aliyah went to first with the news, ashamed to tell her mother for fear of being a disappointment. Somewhere between then and the time Kyle was born, mentor and mentee became best friends. A short time later Lauren's husband, a professor, landed a job at the University of California at Davis, a college located close to where Lauren had grown up. She jumped at the chance to move back west and once she found out about the college's residency program, lobbied for Aliyah to finish there.

After pulling out money for Kyle's entertainment, a move that Lauren summarily rebuffed, Aliyah waved goodbye. Before leaving Lauren's driveway, she typed the address Terrell had texted her into the GPS. He hadn't told her the name of where they were meeting. Not that it mattered. Since arriving a month ago, Aliyah's world had basically been work, home and Kyle's school. Wherever they were meeting was likely someplace she'd not been before.

Fifteen minutes later and not only was she somewhere she'd never been before, but it was also some place she never would have guessed he'd ask her to meet.

Terrell exited his car as she pulled up, his eyes sparkling, smile wide. "Hello, beautiful."

"Hey." She stepped into his open arms for a hug. "What is this place?"

"An airport, Aliyah. Small, I know, but all that we need."

She gave him a look. "Thanks for stating the obvious. Where are we going?"

"San Francisco."

"Are you serious?"

"You said we couldn't meet in Paradise Cove. I couldn't think of an appropriate place for this night in Davis. So we're going to San Francisco."

"And we're flying? I heard it's only an hour's drive away."

"More like ninety minutes, depending on traffic. Why get stuck in traffic when you can fly over it?"

The logic of the rich, much like Kyle's father, except without a snobbish tone. Still, every similarity to Ernest Westcott was a strike against Terrell Drake. But given the emotional distance she planned to maintain, that was probably a good thing.

They entered the regional airport hangar and walked over to a sleek private jet where two men, one casually dressed in button-down and slacks, the other wearing a stained gray uniform, stood talking. Mr. Casual saw them approaching and broke away from the worker, who turned and walked into an office.

"Mr. Drake!"

"Stan, my man!" The two men shook hands. Terrell turned to Aliyah. "Stan, I'd like you to meet Aliyah Robinson, an east coast transplant suffering from a case of small-townitis."

Stan smiled as he held out his hand. "San Francisco is a great remedy for that disease. A pleasure to meet you."

Aliyah greeted him. "Likewise."

"Are we ready to go? I saw you in discussion with the mechanic."

"We were just shooting the breeze. We're all set. Inspection completed. Gauges checked. Bar is stocked. Just waiting on you."

"After you." Terrell stepped aside so that Aliyah could precede him up the steps. Midway, she turned quickly. As expected, his eyes were squarely on her assets.

"Hey, it's directly in my line of vision!"

"You're obsessed," she said with a chuckle, and continued up the steps. Ernest's family had chartered private jets on occasion, for events to which she'd not been invited. This was her first time inside one. If its interior was any indication of how the Drakes lived, theirs was a lavish, luxurious lifestyle. She took it all in: buttery leather seats, mahogany trim, crystal this, platinum that. All the discomfort from earlier returned.

Terrell motioned for Aliyah to sit in one of two front seats, watching her as she did so. "You all right?"

She nodded.

"You're not afraid of flying are you?"

"No, but I'm usually on a bigger plane."

"Don't worry," Terrell said, continuing to the bar that was midway back. "This is one of the safest planes out there and when it comes to pilots, Stan is top-notch. He flew fighter jets in the air force. He can do this hop to San Fran in his sleep. What can I get you to drink?"

"What are you having?"

"Let's pop a bottle—make it a celebration."

"What are we celebrating?"

Terrell shrugged. "Life."

"Sounds good to me."

Terrell poured two flutes and returned to his seat. He lifted his glass. "To a wonderful time in the big city."

Aliyah tapped his glass and sipped. "Mmm, this is good. I don't like champagne that's either too dry or too sweet. This is neither." She took another sip. "What brand is this?"

"It's called Diamond, a Drake Wines product."

Ah, yes. The grape-growing brother. "Your family owns a winery?"

"My immediate family is in real estate, for the most part. But my brother Warren, the one who co-owns the land with my grandfather, planted several acres of grapes that are now thriving. He did so on the advice of one of my cousins, whose family owns a resort and winery in Southern California."

"Lots of success in your family."

"We've been blessed."

The captain walked back and asked them to buckle up. Ten minutes later they were above the clouds that had hovered for most of the day, surrounded by brilliant blue skies and a sun that would not be setting before they landed.

"So tell me about your family, Aliyah."

"It's not like yours, that's for sure."

"Few are." This answer got a raised brow. "I don't say that arrogantly, but honestly. It's a lifestyle that is not commonly experienced, one I'm grateful to have. But nothing was handed to us on a silver platter. My family's achievements come from a combination of luck, good timing and lots of hard work."

Aliyah nodded, her mind awhirl with how to respond to his question. She wasn't ashamed of her family, nor the struggles they all endured growing up in a vibrant but gritty section of Brooklyn's Prospect Heights. The drive, resilience and determination to succeed arose from the notorious neighborhood activities she sometimes witnessed, events that left some childhood friends and acquaintances incarcerated too long, pregnant too young or dead too early. Those experiences helped make her who she was today. But she knew all too well how the upper two percent sometimes viewed the working class, since she'd spent twelve years—high school, undergrad and graduate school—surrounded by students of privilege and families of wealth. While dating Ernest, she had a bird's-eye view of how high society operated—the judgments, condescension and exclusivity, and how friends were chosen less by personality and more by zip code and pedigree. Not even her becoming a doctor was good enough to gain entry. "A charity case to fulfill quotas" was how her attending the same Ivy League college as Ernest was described by his parents. As if her high SAT scores and 4.0 grade average—an average maintained even after the baby and while working part-time—had nothing to do with it.

Terrell mistook her silence. "Listen, Aliyah, I didn't mean to offend you."

"Oh, no. It's not that." She took a sip of champagne and gazed out the window a moment before turning back to him. "Kyle's father is from a wealthy family, one into which I was never accepted. They abhorred my background, disapproved of our dating. My becoming pregnant left them petrified. Their vitriol was unrelenting, to the point where even I questioned my worth. It took a long time to rebuild my confidence. There is evidently still some work to do."

"Where was Kyle's father while his family attacked you?"

Her smile was bittersweet. "Mostly, on their side."

"Even after you gave birth to his son?"

"Oh, that was just to trap him, you see, and a determination made only after paternity was proven by not one official test, but three."

"You can't be serious."

"As serious as his parents were when they demanded I take them. After Kyle was born, they ramped up the pressure for him to dump his low-brow girlfriend and find someone respectable to marry. Someone with the right… credentials. That's what he did."

"Then you're better off without him. A man who doesn't have your back, no matter what the situation or who the person is attacking, doesn't deserve you."

"I appreciate that."

"Hopefully he helps out financially, at least."

"The bare minimum, thanks to creative accounting and a savvy attorney. What they didn't understand, and still don't, is that Ernest's presence in Kyle's life would be more valuable than any check he could write. Every child needs a father, but for boys, it's even more important.

"In the end, it's probably for the best. I wouldn't feel comfortable leaving him alone with that set of grandparents. There's no telling how they'd poison his mind, or scar his soul."

Terrell reached over and caressed her face. "Would it sound too selfish for me to say that I'm glad he's not in your life?"

"Yes, that sounds selfish. But I'm still glad you said it."

He leaned. She leaned. Their lips touched, softly, exploring. Soon their tongues intertwined, still bearing the essence of the wine. He kissed her thoroughly. She matched him stroke for stroke.

He pulled back. "I'd better stop while I can. We'll soon be landing."

Terrell's kiss erased yesteryear's heartache. Aliyah relaxed into the comfort of the supple leather, and began to feel the excitement of being in a private plane with a handsome man, soaring to a night of fun. She finished her flute of champagne and turned flirty eyes to Terrell.

"I'm glad Kyle is at your center. All of the men there, at least the ones I've met, seem genuinely invested in the program's success and are great male role models."

"Including me?"

"Especially you."

Terrell extended his arm across the aisle. Aliyah placed her small hand inside his much larger one. "I'm glad he's there, too. We'll do our best to provide him with the mentorship he needs. Meanwhile, tonight—" Terrell raised her hand and kissed it lightly "—I'd like to make sure his mother, the lovely Aliyah Robinson, gets whatever it is she wants and needs as well."

Chapter 4

They landed at San Francisco International Airport and were whisked away to a cozy, upscale restaurant with stunning views of the bay and the Golden Gate Bridge.

Aliyah looked around. "I didn't expect we'd be someplace this fancy. Glad I wore my crystal stilettos or I'd feel out of place."

"You could walk in here wearing a garbage bag and outshine every woman in the room."

Aliyah laughed and sat back in her chair. "Wow, you are a salesman, aren't you?"

"Yes, and a darn good one. But that wasn't a line."

The waiter came over and after describing the evening's special features, took their drink and appetizer orders. After further discussion of the menu and deciding on entrées, the conversation came back around to their continuing to get to know each other.

"So, Aliyah..."

"Yes?"

"What made you decide to become a doctor?"

"Not just any doctor but an anesthesiologist, specifically. The reason? Shannon's mom."

"Was she an anesthesiologist?"

Aliyah nodded. "My seventh-grade summer, I was selected for a math-and-science program that paired students from different schools to work on a project together. I was paired with this geeky, slightly chubby girl named Shannon. We were best friends from day one. So much so that she invited me to her birthday party. She lived on Manhattan's Upper East Side. That train ride took me to another world and changed my life.

"After that day, I spent several more at her house. One time we were in her room and I was asking how her family lived the way they did. Where they got so much money. Her mother was walking by and answered, 'We worked for it.' I asked her what she did and she told me that she was an anesthesiologist. Right then and there, I decided that's what I'd be, too. Of course, had I known that such a declaration was going to cost me twelve additional years of my life after high school, I would have chosen Shannon's father's career instead."

"What did he do?"

"Worked in finance. On Wall Street. He's retired now. They both are. Shannon still lives in the home I visited but her parents spend most of their time in their villa in France."

"Do you like what you do?"

"I love it. Money and the lavish lifestyle I saw at Shannon's house is what sparked my interest. The satisfaction I found during the educational journey to my goal is what's kept me here."

"You've accomplished a lot. As a single mother, it couldn't have been easy."

"I'm not used to easy. Anytime I think of quitting I remember those on the block who chose differently, and are no longer with us. I never want Kyle to experience what I saw growing up. He's my motivation."

Dinner arrived. The conversation changed. From the appetizer to dessert, the food was as decadent as Aliyah's thoughts had been ever since Terrell's promise to satisfy her. They left the restaurant, and just when she thought the night couldn't get any better Terrell surprised her with tickets and backstage passes to see one of her favorite artists, Janelle Monáe. The show was rocking, so much so that Aliyah was almost able to ignore all the attention Terrell received from the ladies. Even if she were interested in a serious relationship, which she wasn't, Terrell wouldn't be on her short list. Relationships were hard enough. One with walking temptation wrapped around fifty shades of sexy would be impossible.

After spending time with the singer backstage, Terrell placed his arm around Aliyah and pulled her to his side. They walked toward the exit. "Ms. Robinson?"

She placed an arm around his waist. "Yes?"

"Have you enjoyed the evening so far?"

"Are you kidding? This has been the most fun I've had in a long time."

"It makes me happy to hear that."

"I'm happy that you're happy."

He stopped and turned to her. "Then only one question remains."

"What's that?"

"Should our next destination be the airport, to take you home and kiss you good-night at the door, or my place here in San Francisco, away from Paradise Cove's prying eyes?"

She leaned into him. "Mr. Drake, I want you to take me wherever you can fulfill your promise of leaving me fully satisfied."

They couldn't reach the Drake place fast enough.

"Wow." Aliyah stepped inside, immediately noticing the city view from their high perch in the hills. "This is beautiful."

Terrell came up behind her, kissing her temple as he wrapped her in his arms. "So is this."

She turned into him, desire in her eyes. The evidence of his desire was a little farther down.

"You know what I've been wanting to do all night?"

"Probably the same thing on my mind."

Their heads moved in unison toward a mutual destination. The kiss was soft, purposeful, their lips rubbing against each other in a casual get-to-know. Terrell's hands went on a journey of discovery, meandering over her shoulders, down her back and to the top of bootyliciousness. Aliyah, who at five-five had always preferred a tall man, relished how her five-inch heels made it possible to easily wrap her arms around his neck. With a swipe of her tongue against his lips, she intensified the exchange.

He sucked it in, an act that weakened her knees.

After a long moment, they came up for air. Terrell mumbled against her hair, "Damn, you feel good."

"So do you."

"You taste good."

"Mmm."

"I want to taste more of you."

"What are you waiting for?"

He grabbed her hand and led them to the couch. Once seated, he pulled her to his lap. The fit was perfect, as if they'd been designed for each other. The kiss resumed— slower, hotter, wetter. Tongues twirling, slow and easy, hips grinding in the same rhythm. Terrell caressed Aliyah's arm, running his hand down the length of it, coming back up to cup her breast. Seconds more, and he eased down the fabric and palmed the warm flesh beneath. His thumb brushed against a rapidly hardening nipple. Aliyah arched her back, encouraging him to move faster, to take more. Instead he stopped, hugging her tightly before sitting back to look into her eyes.

"What?"

"Girl, I don't know what it is about you. You've got me so turned on!"

"And that's a problem."

"No. I just…"

"Just what."

"I just want to make sure that you're ready for this. That this is what you want."

"You gave me a choice. I'm still happy with the one I made."

"I want you, too. But I don't want something done in the heat of the moment to change how we are with each other. I like you. I want you. But I also respect you. I don't want you to feel bad afterward."

Aliyah rolled off of him and stood. "Look," she began, pulling her top over her head and tossing it on the floor. "We are two clear-thinking, intelligent, consenting adults who came here for the same reason." She reached behind her and unclasped her bra. It joined her top on the floor. Her breasts swayed invitingly, nipples protruding in invitation to be licked. She undid her jeans button and unzipped them before sitting on the couch to remove her shoes. "There will be no regrets, no guilt trips and no expectations. I am as uninterested in a steady relationship as I'm sure you are. Now—" she raised her legs to him "—will you help me take off these jeans and show me what that mouth is good at besides talking?"

She watched his eyes light up and become predatory as he reached for first one leg of her jeans and then the other, removing denim to reveal smooth, flawless skin that reminded him of a favorite childhood drink. Hot chocolate. He stood. She watched. His eyes never left hers as he removed his shoes, shirt and pants. Placing his hands on the band of his boxers, he paused just a moment before pulling them down and stepping out of them in one fluid motion.

"Oh, my goodness," Aliyah cooed, staring unabashedly at eight thick inches of penis perfection. "Is that all for me?"

"All for you, baby. Sit back."

He started at her toes. No preamble, no warning. Just sucked one into his mouth. So nasty, yet so decadently nice. Leisurely placed kisses continued from her ankle to her knee, up the outer and inner sides of thigh. She spread her legs in invitation, though there was none needed. His index finger was already working itself between her thong's elastic edge, already teasing her moistening folds as his tongue teased the slip of satin covering her treasure. Aliyah hissed and moaned, swirling her hips against his tongue to increase the friction and douse her desire.

Her actions were rewarded when Terrell slipped his tongue beneath the thong and kissed the satin of her skin. Lapping, nipping, licking, tasting her over and again. Aliyah threw back her head in ecstasy. The man was a maestro, playing her passion with precision and skill. Sweet torture that she wanted to stop, that she hoped would go on forever.

But she wanted more.

"Stand up."

No answer. His tongue was busy doing other things. She chuckled, placed her hands on the sides of his head and gently pulled him away from her. "Stand up."

"What's wrong?"

"Just do it."

He complied. In an instant Aliyah was on her knees, fondling the massive weapon that had made her mouth water. She licked its length, outlined the perfect mushroom tip with her tongue, took him in, slowly, fully.

"Aliyah." Spoken like a promise, or a prayer. "Baby…" He pulled back. "You're driving me crazy. I've got to be inside you, now."

He reached for protection and then sat on the couch. Aliyah climbed on top of him and slowly, oh, so slowly, eased down on his massive shaft, allowing the delicious friction to heat up her insides. He pulled a nipple into his mouth and reverently cupped the butt that began this journey. Squeezing. Kneading. Grinding. Thrusting. Hard and fast, then slow and easy. Riding one wave of ecstasy after another, resting only long enough to ride again.

Later, they moved to the master suite, where the vastness of the four-poster, king-size bed offered a whole new realm of possibilities. They explored them all, each matching the other's voracious appetite with their own unbridled enthusiasm. Each had clearly met their match.

When Aliyah returned to earth from a shattering climax that brought her near tears, she cuddled in the crook of Terrell's arm, listening as his own heartbeat slowed and returned to normal.

"Terrell."

"Yes, Ms. Robinson."

"That was frickin' amazing."

He laughed, pulled her even closer. "So you're saying I took care of you properly?"

"Yeah, you were all right." Said in that lazy, drawn-out way she'd heard the teens do it.

This answer lifted his head from the pillow. "Just all right?"

"Yes." He grunted. She smiled into the darkness, doubting his sexual prowess had been called anything less than amazing his entire life. If indeed it had happened, whoever said it had lied. "Terrell?"

"Yes, Aliyah."

"Can you be all right again in the morning?"

His deep-throated chuckle was the last thing she heard before falling asleep.

Chapter 5

He awoke to her lips kissing his manhood, her glory spread before him like a gourmet buffet.

"Good morning!" he said.

She purred, occupied.

"You sure know how to wake a man up."

She knew how to do more than that. Working magic with her tongue and fingers caused all talk to cease until after they'd showered. After drying off, they strode down the stairs in their toned, naked glory and retrieved the clothes that last night had been tossed aside.

Terrell reached for his boxers. "What do you want for breakfast?" She wriggled her eyebrows suggestively. "Girl, stop!"

"Ha!"

"Dang! I never thought I'd meet someone who liked sex more than I do."

"I would apologize for wearing you out but truthfully, I'm not at all sorry." She zipped up her jeans and reached for her bra. "It had been a while."

"I could tell."

"Shut up!"

They laughed, sharing a comfortable camaraderie that some couples never experienced, even after being together for years.

"Seriously, though. What do you feel like eating?"

"Something quick. I want to spend the afternoon with Kyle."

"Hey, why don't the two of you come over for brunch?"

"You cook?"

He put up his hands. "Oh, no. I'm allergic to the kitchen. I'm talking about coming over to my parents' house, where we have brunch every Sunday."

She smiled. "No, thank you."

"Why not?"

"Um, this isn't a meeting-the-family kind of situation, remember?"

"Oh, no. It's not like that. Friends get invited over all the time."

She gave him a look. "Even more reason not to be woman number whatever showing up."

"Wait! Not those kinds of friends."

"Then what kinds of friends?"

"Friends who I really like. Not just anyone. I don't invite booty calls over to my mama's house, for instance."

"Something tells me that to do that your mama would have to have a really big house."

"Ha!"

"I appreciate the invite but would rather grab something quick and casual on the way to the airport. Are we leaving now?"

"Wow, she uses me all night long, wrings every ounce of strength from my body, then tosses me aside with the first light of morning."

"No, I used you some more at the first light of morning. It's almost ten o'clock." Sliding on her shoe, she walked over and gave him a peck on the lips. "I'm going to use the restroom and then I'll be ready to go."

Terrell reached for his phone to call the pilot, shaking his head as he watched Aliyah leave the room.

A short time later they arrived at the airport, takeout

orders from an organic café in hand. Stan greeted them cheerfully. "Breakfast for me? Terrell, you shouldn't have."

"Good. Because I didn't." They laughed. "Give me a minute to heat this up and get situated, all right?"

"Sure. Just let me know when you're ready."

Ten minutes later they were in the air, speeding toward Paradise Cove...and reality.

"That was delicious." Aliyah finished off the last of her egg white omelet and swiped her mouth with a napkin. "Everything about this weekend was oh-so tasty!" She reached over and placed a hand on Terrell's arm. "Thanks again for inviting me out. It was just the date I needed. The last few months have been busy—securing the job, finding a house, moving across country. And that's after a jam-packed schedule, four years of killer courses to get my degree." She sighed, looked away. "And everything else." A second, and then she turned back to him. "I didn't realize how long it had been since I totally relaxed and enjoyed myself. But I was able to do that with you."

"I'm happy that you're happy, and enjoyed myself as well."

She pulled out her phone and they were both soon busy texting, answering messages and emails that last night had been ignored. Casual conversation flowed in between, making the forty-five-minute flight back home seem much shorter.

They landed. He walked her to her car, shared a quick kiss and hug. Terrell opened her door. "I'll see you tomorrow, right?"

"How so?"

"Your son. The center. Our tutoring and activity program?"

"Actually, no. I came to enroll him and scope out the place. Since everything I saw met with my approval—"

she paused, giving him a slow once-over "—Lauren, his babysitter, will likely handle it from here on out."

"Then when am I going to see you?"

"Soon." She got into her car, gave a quick wave and was gone. He watched her car turn on to the street and speed away, and wondered why his heart seemed to go with her.

He knew just who to call for the answer, and wasn't surprised when just as he thought this, his phone rang. That whole twin-radar, two-halves-of-the-same-whole sort of thing. He tapped the speaker button. "Tee."

"Hey, Tee." It was his sister, Teresa.

"I was just getting ready to call you."

"I know. What kind of trouble have you gotten yourself into this weekend?"

"No trouble, sis."

"That's not the vibe I'm getting. Who is she?"

"The mother of one of the new students at the center. Her name is Aliyah."

"All right, Silky."

"Ha!" It had been a while since Terrell had heard this high school nickname. "What made you call me that?"

"Hearing that Cindy was divorced and living back in PC. Remember that cheer she made up after hearing that was your nickname?" She adopted a high-pitched voice. "Terrell Drake, with all the moves, a voice like silk and twice as smooth."

"Please, sis. Spare me the memory. Crazy that you brought it up, though. I ran in to her while meeting Aliyah for dinner."

"Was she pushy, as usual?"

"She basically invited herself to join us for dinner. What would you call it?"

"Ha! Cindy was in love with Silky."

"Girl, stop."

"What about the rule we made? Don't reach where you teach!"

"I wasn't reaching."

"What, she kidnapped you?"

"She gave me a second chance to make a first impression, which led to a third one."

"What was her first impression? Never mind, just start at the beginning and tell me everything."

"Well, sis, it all started when I turned the corner and saw this wonderful behind."

"Oh, Lord."

"Perfectly proportioned on this amazing body."

"And you just had to have her phone number."

"As one of the center's volunteer faculty, it was my duty to follow up on the new enrollee and make sure all had been handled properly. That's all…"

"Oh, so that's what was on your mind? Duty? I thought it was booty."

Terrell could only laugh at the truth. He continued, filling her in on how he got busted and why he felt he at least owed her dinner. How cool and down to earth Aliyah was and how conversation flowed.

"Before the first date was over, I knew I wanted a second one. She did, too, but not in Paradise Cove."

"With Cindy's tactless antics, who could blame her?"

"I was glad she felt that way."

"Unlike all the others in PC, who'd make sure your date was somewhere public where everybody would know they'd been with a Drake."

"Well, you know."

"Unfortunately, yes, I do."

Terrell chuckled. "Anyway, last night we went to San Francisco. Dinner, concert, a night on the hill. I'm driving home from the airport now."

"Sounds like a top-tier Drake date. What didn't she like?"

"She loved it. Said it was the best time she'd had in a while."

"Oh, so now you're afraid she'll stalk you at the center, wanting exclusivity?"

"No, exactly the opposite. She made it clear that this was just a sex thing, basically—wouldn't even accept my invitation to Sunday brunch."

"Wow, Tee, she sounds like you!"

"I knew you'd say that."

"Because it's true!"

"The way she dismissed me, so casually, made me feel like a used piece of meat. I need to call every girl I sent home after the deed was done and apologize."

"No apology needed if that's all they expected. Clearly that's what your girl thought last night. But from the sound of your voice and the words left unspoken, you might be the one who ends up stalking her!"

"Tee?"

"What?"

"Go wrestle a bear."

"Ha! I love you, too. And for the record while I've grown to love Alaska, I'm still afraid of the wild."

"No matter what, Tee, you'll always be city. I need to run. Tell Atka I said what's up."

"Will do."

Chapter 6

Aliyah signed out of her FaceTime account, happy that she'd been able to see and speak to her whole family. These days, finding her parents and four siblings all home at the same time was rare. It made her miss New York, but it also allowed her to see that all of her hard work was paying off. She hadn't gone to college and blazed a trail of success just for herself. She'd done it so that the four hardheads looking up to her—three brothers and one sister, all younger—could have a clear example of how to avoid life's pitfalls and go for one's dreams. The two oldest brothers were excelling in college. The younger brother and sister still made her nervous, entranced by the smoke and mirrors of quick money and instant success. Gangs constantly courted her six-foot-plus brother. Pretty-boy tough guys wanted to date her gorgeous sixteen-year-old sister. Avoiding neighborhood temptations was hard. But so far, they'd succeeded.

After a final check on Kyle, Aliyah turned out the lights and climbed into a bed that suddenly felt too big and too empty. She'd stayed busy on purpose, had filled her entire day with one project or event after another. All to keep her mind occupied and not think of Terrell. But now, with the house quiet, and her lying down, images and memories of San Francisco assailed her. She couldn't ignore them as she'd done to Terrell's earlier phone call. Thinking of the message he'd left made her tingle and smile at the same time. It was simple. Three words. They'd thrummed like a mantra in her head all day.

I want more.

She did, too. And she planned to get it, as much as she could. Hands down, he was the best she'd ever even dreamed about having. If he were a drug, she'd need rehab. Already. After just a few days. So she needed to find a way to assuage her appetite while guarding her heart. She wasn't looking for commitment. If she were, someone like Terrell Drake would not be a likely candidate. It's why she'd never considered a serious relationship with her childhood friend, turned lover. He was tall, handsome and virile, with enough charisma to fill the Atlantic—characteristics that were great for a good time and a roll in the hay. Not the best for a committed relationship. She never worried about Ernest. Turned out he was an arrogant, superficial, self-centered a-hole. But as far as she knew, he was faithful. Even jerks could have one good trait.

She changed positions, fluffed her pillow and settled down in search of sleep. As it came, the mantra continued.

I want more.

The next morning, Aliyah's phone rang at 7:00 a.m. Given her family lived on the east coast, this was not an unusual occurrence. She reached over, eyes still closed, and answered.

"Hello?"

"Good morning, Ms. Robinson."

Her eyes flew open. "Terrell?"

"I wish I could say I'm sorry for waking you up, but what I really feel bad about is that I'm not there with you."

"You're such a playboy," she said with a chuckle, rolling over and getting out of bed. She left the room in search of tea.

"Is that what I am?"

"Absolutely."

"What makes you say that?"

"Where do I start? It could be that woman-magnet sports car you drive. Or the daggers shot at me by every woman who saw us together in the Cove Café. Or better yet, what about the woman who invited herself to our table?"

"Hey…"

"No, wait, I'm not done. Let's not leave out the lover's lair you own in San Francisco and perhaps in other major cities as well. Lastly, add a handsome face, a killer bod and skills in the bedroom and you have all the attributes of the perfect player."

A pause and then, "Are you done now?"

"Yes, I believe so."

"Good. Because your reasoning is skewed."

"How so?"

"Just because a man takes care of himself and has nice things doesn't mean he's a playboy. As for what happened in the café, that's just small-town nosiness and Cindy being Cindy.

"Yours was a new, unrecognized face in a town where everyone knows everybody, and everyone wants to know my business. Your being with me made you my business. I'm sure the grapevine is still buzzing with questions about who you are."

"Hmm."

"And for the record, the house in San Francisco is not my lair. It is a family property. We all stay there when in town, as do some of our friends and colleagues. However, I do not apologize for being particularly fond of the opposite sex, and especially interested in the one I'm talking to right now, the one who didn't return my call from yesterday."

"Terrell, it's early in the morning. You hardly gave me a chance."

"Whenever you see my number on the screen, you are to call me back immediately."

"Oh, is that so?"

"Yes, it is."

"Or what?"

"Or I'm going to come over and spank you just right, and love you 'til you holler and throw up both your hands."

She laughed. "Don't you have to be at work or something?"

"I'm already here. What about you? Are your hours as erratic as I hear they can be for medical doctors?"

"Right now, even more so. Tuesday through Thursday I'm in residency at UC Davis Medical Center, then I intern at a local hospital, Living Medical, on Monday and Friday. And there's still studying to do on top of all that. Which is why this past weekend was so appreciated."

"Wow. No wonder you're not interested in a relationship. You don't have time for one."

"Exactly."

"Well, guess what?"

"What?"

"You need to make some time for yours truly. I need to finish what I started in San Francisco."

"Which was?"

"Satisfying you."

"Oh, trust me, you did that."

"Baby, that was just the appetizer. I want the whole meal."

"Well, unless you're up for a midnight rendezvous in a hotel near the hospital, your dining will to have to wait."

"Until when?"

"Um…next Sunday?"

"All right."

"All right, fine. I've got to run and wake the kid but

I'll call you toward the end of the week, make sure we're still on."

"See you soon."

Aliyah got Kyle dressed and took him out for his favorite pancake breakfast. While they ate, however, it was Terrell's appetite that was on her mind. He was successful, an expert lover and could charm the panties off most women. She'd love to pursue something with him. But the timing was all wrong. She was at the beginning of at least two and a half years of intense residency training. At the most, she'd have time for a little tune-up every once and again, but real dates? Like the one they'd just had? Unlikely. Something told her Terrell wouldn't be happy with that. To her, he seemed like a man who wanted lots of attention. And lots of sex.

At least they had one thing in common.

Chapter 7

Terrell leaned against the doorjamb, watching his friend since high school, Luther, playfully interacting with a group of five- and six-year-old boys. They used to wreak havoc in the clubs, engaging ladies who wanted to be with them and angering men who wanted to be them. Since getting married and having children, Luther had gone from tough guy to teddy bear. Terrell was proud of his friends and business partners who'd stepped up to the plate and agreed to be mentors and role models for the young men who came to the center, many of whose fathers were absent, deployed or incarcerated. Luther was the perfect one to handle the little ones. Terrell mentored the teens.

All except one young boy, whom he looked for now. Kyle was seated on a mat, surrounded by Legos, using his imagination to create something grand.

Terrell stepped into the room and after a brief chat with Luther walked over to where Kyle was playing and kneeled down.

"Hey, little man."

"I'm not little." This said while remaining focused on the task at hand. "I'm big."

"Oh, all right. Excuse my error." In this moment, Terrell realized just how infrequent he interacted with people under the age of ten and, thinking of his nieces and nephews, over the age of two. Terrell found himself in the rare position of being at a loss for words. But he'd told Aliyah that he'd take special interest in, and mentor, her son. He was a man of his word. So he placed down the deck of math flash cards he'd used earlier with the teens, sat beside Kyle and picked up a bright red block.

"What are you building?"

"A trajectory."

"A what?"

Kyle repeated what he said.

"A trajectory is a direction, Kyle, not an object." To this Kyle remained silent. "Although I am impressed that you know the word." He took the red block he was holding. "May I?" Kyle nodded. Terrell added the block to Kyle's "trajectory."

Kyle looked over at the flash cards Terrell had put down. "What are these?"

"Math quizzes."

"Let me see!"

"Naw, these are for teenagers—a little too much for someone your age. Can you count, though?"

"Of course." Kyle gave him a look that reminded him so much of Aliyah that Terrell laughed. He reached for one of the flash cards Terrell set down and watched Kyle pretend to add the numbers, silently mouthing figures as his fingers tapped the floor. Terrell reached for his vibrating phone. Meeting reminder. Time to go.

"Good talking to you, Kyle. May I have my cards back?"

"Can I keep them?"

"No, those are for the big, I mean older, boys." Kyle returned the flash cards. "Take care, little man."

"'Bye."

The day passed quickly and the next two were a blur. Between work at Drake Realty, mentoring at Drake Center, board meetings and social networking, Terrell barely managed to squeeze in time to sleep. And he hadn't talked to Aliyah. He'd gotten voice mail when he called yesterday and missed her call last night. But he knew she got off work tonight at eleven. And that was why at nine thirty he was in his car and headed to Davis. He would be waiting by her car when she got off work, ready to help her relax.

When it was something or someone he wanted, Terrell was a persistent man.

He surfed the web to pass the time. Unlike the rest of the week, tonight time seemed to pass slowly. Finally at eleven fifteen he saw her, looking tired but lovely. A pair of scrubs had never looked so good. His heart flip-flopped. He ignored it. This wasn't the first gorgeous woman he'd dated. Nor the most successful. The newness of their being together was why he was so excited to see her. That was his story and he was sticking to it.

He quietly got out of his car. She didn't see him. He began walking toward her. She didn't even look up. When he was about three feet away, he spoke to her. "Hey, Ms. Robinson."

She jumped, eyes wide, her hand to her throat. "Terrell?! Oh, my gosh! You scared me to death."

"I didn't mean to." He opened his arms. She stepped into his embrace. "It's a good thing I wasn't the bad guy. You would have been caught totally off guard."

"I just did seventeen hours," she said with a yawn, stepping away from him to look in his face. "What are you doing here?"

"I couldn't get you on the phone so I came over."

"'Over,'" she said, using air quotes for emphasis, "is thirty miles away."

"You know what they say. Ain't no mountain high enough."

She stepped around him and continued to her car. He fell into step beside her. "I wish you'd called first. I'm exhausted. The only thing in my immediate future is a bed and a pillow."

"That's fine. I just want to share it with you."

She looked at her watch. "At this time of night, Kyle is the only male allowed in my home."

"That's no problem. We can do what you suggested earlier and get a hotel room. With a king-size bed."

"Terrell…" She reached for her door handle. He placed his hand on top of hers.

"You don't have to do anything but go to sleep."

"You came all this way to watch me sleep."

"No, but—"

"Exactly. And that's all I'm going to do and even that for only four or five hours. My three days here are always intense. I'm back on the clock at six thirty."

"Dang. That's hard work."

"Sorry."

"Since I'm here, though, I might as well stay—right? We can do your apartment or a hotel. All you have to do is sleep, unless—" he took a step toward her, massaged the nape of her neck "—you get a spurt of energy and want to do something else."

"You forget I have a son to pick up from Lauren's house."

"Didn't you tell me her son was Kyle's age? Ask if he can spend the night."

She eyed him a minute and shrugged. "Okay, but don't say I didn't warn you."

"Where are we going?"

"There's a Westin right down the street. Let's go there. Follow me."

He did and within fifteen minutes they were in the room and in the shower, Aliyah allowing the water to cascade down her hair and face.

"My baby's so tired." Terrell poured a generous amount of liquid soap on the washcloth, rubbing it in a circular motion across her skin. The result was bubbles all over her body, which he began to wash off. When she yawned again, he finished the work quickly, turned off the shower and wrapped her in a towel. "Let's go to bed."

They lay down. Aliyah rolled to her side, adjusting the pillow as she did. "Thank you for coming, Terrell. Good night."

"Good night," he said, spooning behind her, his mind swimming with ideas of how good the night was going to get.

He placed his hand on her naked hip, massaging gently. Her skin was warm and velvety soft. His semi-erection hardened as he rubbed his hand down her thigh, around to her luscious booty and up to her waist.

Aliyah murmured something, reached for his hand to pull his arm tighter around her and nestled deeper under the cover.

Terrell smiled. *Yeah, I've still got it. Sleepy? I'll take care of that.*

He moved in with kisses—neck, back, arm. Rolled her over. She didn't resist. "Um, Terrell…"

"Shh, just lay back and enjoy, baby."

More kisses—tender, feathery, a purposeful trail from her breasts to her navel and continuing on to her hips and thighs. He repositioned himself, spread her legs and French-kissed her pleasure lips. He heard a whimper. Felt he would have her screaming his name in five minutes or less. He licked, kissed and tantalized her with her fingers.

There it was again. That sound.

He stopped. Listened. Looked.

What he thought was a whimper was in fact a soft snore. Aliyah was sound asleep.

Terrell fell back on the bed, stunned. Here he was pulling out all the stops, being Mr. Player, Terrell the Torrential

Lover, and she goes to sleep? In answer, another soft snore and then quiet, as she turned back on her side.

If his friends ever found out about this they'd never let him forget it, and that was why no one save he and Aliyah would ever know. He'd have to pull his player card for real.

Aliyah wasn't the only one who got a surprise tonight.

Chapter 8

Seemed her head had just hit the pillow when the soft chimes of her alarm announced that sleep time was over. Aliyah gently removed Terrell's arm from around her waist, scooted out of bed and headed to the shower. If she hurried, she could get coffee and food, both sorely needed, before her shift started.

The spray of cold water blasted away sleep. She turned it to warm and began a quick shower. Halfway through, her hand stopped in midair. A dream, fuzzy and incomplete, came to mind. An image of Terrell, kissing, teasing, loving her orally. The mere thought caused her nipples to pebble and her core to clench. She shook away the mental picture and turned off the water. A day in bed with her skillful lover wasn't going to happen, no matter how much she wished it could.

"Good morning." Terrell came in and hugged Aliyah from behind.

"Morning." Aliyah wriggled out of his embrace, gave Terrell's lips a quick peck and hurried out of the bathroom. "I hate to rush you but can we leave in five? I'd like to grab breakfast before my shift starts."

"Right away, Doctor."

"Said with a hint of sarcasm." She pulled on her scrubs, pulling her hair into a ponytail as she stepped into the bathroom doorway. "I'm sorry it's so busy. If given the option,

I'd much rather spend the day with you and that weapon poking me in the back last night."

"Please, girl." He left the bathroom and began dressing. "You didn't feel a thing."

"That's because we didn't do anything, even though I dreamed otherwise."

"What did you dream?"

"That you were…never mind. I've got to go."

"Call me from your car. I want to hear about this dream you had."

"Okay." She headed for the door.

"If you don't, I'm coming back to the hospital."

"You're a brat."

"Call me."

Once out of the parking lot, Aliyah called him.

"Okay…back to the dream," he said, instead of hello.

"I'm a little embarrassed. I dreamed that we were having oral sex…well, you were doing it to me and—"

"That wasn't a dream."

"Huh?"

"I came to bed, all prepared to get you relaxed, make you feel good, make long and slow love to you."

"And?"

"And you fell asleep with my tongue in your—"

"No!"

"Passed out. Zonked. It was a wrap."

"Stop playing!"

"I was serious, too, down there getting it in!" Aliyah laughed, not believing him for a minute. "I heard you moaning and I was like, 'yeah, I'm going to tear this up.' Then I listened. I think you're all into it. But I stop, listen again. You weren't moaning. You were snoring."

"Ha!"

Terrell tried to remain quiet but soon he laughed, too.

"Good thing I'm a confident man because a woman falling asleep in the middle of the act is quite the ego deflator."

"Babe, I was exhausted! I told you!"

"I know, but…"

"Oh, gosh! I can just about imagine your face…" Laughter swallowed up the rest of her sentence.

"Gee. Thanks a lot."

"I'm sorry."

"You don't sound sorry."

"But I am." She tried to hold it in but imagining the look on his face when he discovered she was snoring instead of moaning made her burst out laughing again.

"That's alright. Payback will come later. Hey, are you off on Halloween?"

"Yes, why?"

"An event in PC. I'll call you later about it."

After a quick date with a drive-thru, Aliyah returned to the UC Davis Medical Center. At the nurses' station, she checked the charts to confirm what was scheduled, then went to see her first patient of the day.

"Good morning, Mr. Robinson!"

"There's my beautiful wife!"

Said with blue eyes twinkling. Ever since eighty-two-year-old widower Dale Robinson had learned they shared the same last name, he'd insisted she was the one he'd searched for all his life. He was dealing with a debilitating back injury in a place too risky for surgery. The doctor's recommendation had been a positive attitude and pain medication. Dale had loads of the former. The latter was where Aliyah's knowledge of pain management kicked in. If it made this nice old man feel better for a few moments, then she'd gladly be his wifey through every treatment.

"Sounds like someone is feeling better this morning!"

"Always feel better when you're here, hon."

"Aww, that's nice." She reached for his wrist, checked his pulse and body temperature.

"Am I alive?"

"Absolutely."

"Well, praise the Lord."

She smiled at his humor. "How's the pain today?"

"Fair to middling."

"Good enough for us to hold off on treatment for a bit? I can handle a few other patients and come back if you'd like."

"Why don't you do that—as soon as that syrup hits my system it knocks me out, cuts into my flirting time."

"Well, we can't have that now, can we?"

"Looks like I'm not the only one in a good mood today. Is somebody trying to step in and steal you away from me?"

"Who could do that?" Aliyah lightly replied, as her mind brought up an image of what Terrell had said was happening when she fell asleep. And how it felt to walk out and see him waiting: wanting, needing, to see her. In that moment, she knew the answer. Because Terrell made her feel significant.

Later that afternoon, because of a multicar accident, Aliyah got the opportunity to first shadow and later assist the anesthesiologist on duty in emergency. The rest of the day went quickly. For that she was grateful. Fridays at Living Medical were usually slow and easy, aided by the fact that tomorrow she worked the afternoon shift, noon to eight, with a chance of getting off early. With Halloween approaching, she hoped Davis citizens stayed healthy so she could be Mommy and spend the day with Kyle.

Once off work and on her way to pick up Kyle, she called Terrell.

"Hello, Doctor."

She laughed. "That sounds weird."

"Well, that's the title you're busting your butt for so get used to it."

"Earlier you mentioned an event in PC?"

"Yes."

"What is it?"

She listened, skillfully navigating the rush-hour traffic and arriving at Lauren's in no time. After ending the call she walked up the drive, rang the bell and then walked in through a door that during the day was often left unlocked.

"Lauren, it's me!"

Lauren came around the corner. "I thought I heard someone pull up. Come on in. The boys are having dinner, which was delayed a bit because we stopped at the mall."

"No worries."

"You hungry?"

"A little. What'd you cook?"

"Two large supreme with extra pepperoni."

Aliyah laughed. "I'll have a slice." She followed Lauren to the dining room, where Conrad, Cody, Conner and Kyle were debating God knew what between bites. "Hi, guys."

Mumbled greetings from filled mouths echoed around the table.

"Mommy—" Kyle began.

"Don't talk with your mouth full, Kyle." He hurriedly finished his bite. "Don't swallow food without chewing, either."

"Sorry, Mommy. But, listen. I helped Conrad do his homework!"

"Let's have wine with the pizza," Lauren yelled from the kitchen.

"That's nice, son. Mommy's going to talk with Miss Lauren." She walked into the kitchen and was greeted by a full glass of wine and a plate for her pizza.

"Let's go in the other room." Lauren's tone was serious. "We need to talk."

"Ooh, okay."

"No messes, boys, and no fighting."

"Where you going, Mommy?"

"Miss Lauren and I are going to have a grown-up chat."

The two women walked by just as Lauren's professor husband, Calvin, walked through the door. After quick greetings and being informed he was now on kid patrol, he continued to the dining room while Lauren and Aliyah continued to the stylish yet lived-in den of the Hensleys's rambling ranch-styled home and sat on the oversize sectional dominating the far corner.

Aliyah took a few sips of wine. The tone in Lauren's voice made her think that she might need it. "Okay, girl. What's going on?"

"Uh, hello. That's what I'm here to ask you?"

Aliyah was genuinely confused. Then it hit her. "Oh. The date."

"Oh, the date," Lauren mocked. "The date, first one mind you—"

"Second, technically—"

"Not according to you Ms. It's Just Dinner."

Aliyah could only laugh. She was guilty as charged.

"First date with a near stranger where you were flown via private plane to San Francisco and did who knows what since the person who thought she was your BFF hasn't been told a thing!"

Lauren's expressiveness had grown more animated with each word, causing Aliyah to laugh harder. "It's a shame you didn't pursue that acting career. You've could have gone places."

"But not to San Francisco on a private with a hunk."

"I'm sorry. I've been meaning to tell you, really, but you know how busy it's been." Aliyah took another sip of wine, then set down the glass. "So, I told you about the dinner in Paradise Cove, right?"

"Only that some woman tried to invite herself to join you."

"Okay. Well…"

For the next fifteen minutes, Lauren sat spellbound as Aliyah recalled her magical date with Terrell, their steamy phone conversations and his surprising her at work after she'd finished her shift.

Lauren's mouth dropped. "You told me you were working late, that's why you wanted Kyle to stay overnight!"

Aliyah wriggled her brows. "I was."

The ladies cracked up.

"So when do I get to meet this Drake fella?"

Aliyah reached for her phone, went to the internet and pulled up his image. "Here he is."

"Hot damn!" Lauren whooped. "Girl, now I really understand. You were working late!"

"He just invited me to spend Halloween in Paradise Cove, to attend a festival they're having. I don't know if I'm going."

"Why not?"

"Several reasons. One, his family will be there. Two, I'll have Kyle, and three, I don't want to blur the lines and confuse him. He already thinks Mr. Drake is 'cool.'" She used air quotes. "He doesn't need to know that his mommy has the hots for Mr. Cool."

Lauren looked again at his photo. "He is a hottie. I have to agree with you on that."

"You and half the women in this state. All he and I will ever have is a casual, mutually pleasurable…friendship."

"All the more reason to join him on the 31st. Let him be your boo."

"On that really tired note…" Both women laughed as Aliyah stood. "It's getting late. I should go and get Kyle in bed."

Lauren stood as well, and put her arm around Aliyah's

shoulders as they walked out together. "It's good to see you happy, girl. You deserve it. And though you haven't asked, here's a piece of advice."

"Oh, no."

They stopped just beyond the living room, where the boys were now playing video games. Lauren turned to Aliyah. "Don't be so quick to define this situation. I know why you're doing it, and I understand. Just try not to let the past shape your present and impact your future. Okay?"

Aliyah slowly nodded. "Okay."

After sitting and chatting for a while with the family, she and Kyle left the Hensley clan and spent a quiet evening at home. They munched on popcorn while watching a movie and topped the snack off with homemade shakes. After Kyle was in bed and her studying was done, she lay listening to music to fall asleep, Aliyah continued to think about what Lauren said. Ernest was her past. Could Terrell be her future? From her point of view, not likely. But he was her present, so for now, she'd just enjoy the gift.

Chapter 9

A light tap on his office door caused Terrell to look up from the computer screen. It was his brother Ike. He leaned back against the chair. "You out of here, man?"

"Yeah, I think I'm done for the day."

"A rare night that you beat me out of here."

"A rare night that you stay late."

"Hey, I'm efficient, what can I say?"

"You can say what really happened, that you're still here because you were late this morning." Ike stepped into the office and sat in a chair in front of Terrell's desk. "Mom said she thought you were dating someone new."

"Mom thinks and says too much."

Ike laughed. "True that." A pause and then he asked, "It isn't Cindy, is it? I heard she's back in town."

"Unfortunately."

"You've seen her?"

"Briefly."

"Silky, Silky!"

"Ha! What is it about Cindy that makes y'all remember Silky? Teresa did the same thing!"

"Probably because she got on my nerves with it. It's really a compliment, just so you know. Your gift of gab and salesmanship."

"And my way with women, that's mostly how it was used."

"That, too. So who is it?"

"A new friend with benefits."

"Another one? Variety might be the spice of life, but when it comes to those beneficial friends you collect like souvenir shot glasses, there might be such a thing as too many."

"I'm not that bad."

"You're worse?"

"Ha!"

Terrell reached for the water bottle on his desk and rocked back in the leather office recliner. "Actually, between the workload here and activities at the center, I don't have much time to mess around."

"I've been meaning to get over there, put in a few volunteer hours."

"You should. I balked at first but working with those young men feels good. That first week they acted like knuckleheads but I got them in line quick, let them know I wasn't playing and that the rules of the center—mutual respect, nonviolent resolution, circumspect conduct—weren't up for debate. The scowls remained for a little while, but after a few days everything mellowed out. May have been the first time some of them had been man-handled, you know what I mean?" Ike nodded. "I think they appreciate it."

"Coming up the way we did, with both our father and grandfather being such huge influences in our lives, and some uncles even, I can't imagine coming into manhood without that male support, those role models."

"Exactly. That's what makes me feel good about it."

"You sure it isn't that one student's bootylicious mama you've been seeing?"

Terrell's mouth dropped. Busted. "Dang, man! First Mom, now Teresa, too?"

"Don't be mad at her," Ike said amid laughter. "Mom

is the one who pried it out of her. I just happened to be over to the house."

Terrell shook his head, smiling, too. "Can't keep a secret in this family for nothing!"

"It's pretty tough." Ike stood. "Well, man, I'm out of here."

"All right, bro. Oh, and Ike?"

"Yes?"

"You're looking old, man. Looks like you could use a little bootylicious yourself."

His cell phone rang as Ike left the office. Bootylicious was calling. "Hey, you."

"You sound happy."

"I was just teasing my brother. Where are you?"

"In bed."

"So early? You feeling okay?"

"Just tired but that's nothing new. Those three days always leave me exhausted."

"The residency at the medical center, correct?"

"That's the one."

"And then you're somewhere else the other two days."

"At Living Medical, a center for the aging and disabled. I'm always studying, but on Saturdays it's a priority. Sunday is reserved for quality time with Kyle. Though she's a dear friend, I feel bad he spends so much time with his sitter, Lauren, and her family."

"What you're doing is to help secure his future. He'll thank you in the end."

"I hope so."

"Maybe I should come over and keep you company."

"Trust me, company is the last thing I need right now. Unless you want a repeat of last night."

"Go ahead. I hear you laughing."

"I'm not!" She was.

"Make a brother feel bad!"

"I felt awful, I really did. You know if there'd been any energy in me at all, I would not have turned you down."

"Is that right?"

"With that magic wand you're working with? Absolutely not!"

Terrell lowered his voice. "Well, my magic wand wants to perform a trick or two on you. Tonight."

"You're so bad. Terrell, I'm exhausted. Plus, I wouldn't want you to come over with Kyle home. He's very observant and very talkative, if you know what I mean. If he saw you over here tonight, trust me, everyone at the center would know about it tomorrow."

"Whoa, then you're right. Not the best idea."

"I thought you'd see things my way."

"Then what about the Halloween festival? It's on a Sunday. That's perfect, right? We could spend the day together."

"Thanks, Terrell, but no, I'll pass. Like I said earlier, I want to spend more time with Kyle so whatever I do will involve him, too."

"By all means. There's a big celebration planned by the lake. There will be activities and fun for people of all ages." No comment. "Oh, right, can't have Mr. Big Mouth spreading our business."

"Hey, that's my son you're talking about!"

They laughed. Terrell glanced at his watch and fired up his sleeping computer once more. "Look, I'm still at work and need to finish up."

"No worries."

"You need to change your mind and spend Halloween with me."

"Look, don't get dictatorial."

"I thought that's the part you loved about me."

"Ha! You're silly. 'Bye, Terrell."

"Goodbye, Aliyah."

Terrell went back to work, thinking of wands, magic tricks and how he couldn't wait to spend time with Aliyah.

Chapter 10

This year, Halloween fell on a Sunday. A good thing, except if she'd had a choice, Aliyah would have happily spent the day in bed with a remote in one hand and a bag of junk food in the other. But for mothers of hyper five-year-olds, this was not an option. So she sat at the computer, checking out the festivities happening in Davis. Not much. She clicked over to Paradise Cove's website. A list of events jumped off the page. Scrolling down, she saw the Drake Lake event Terrell had invited her to attend. Listed were games, pony rides, a treasure hunt, face painting and more, things that Kyle would truly enjoy. Topping all of that off was a haunted house tour and Halloween costume contest. Was it right to deny her son a good time because of her insecurities and bad memories? There would probably be hundreds of people there. Chances were she wouldn't even see his family. As for his female fan club, which she was sure would be circling, that was more his problem than hers.

She reached for her cell. He answered on the second ring. "I've changed my mind."

"About what?"

"About accepting your invitation."

"That's great, babe. What made you change your mind?"

"The list of activities listed on the PC website. I thought

to also invite my friend Lauren and her family. Her boys will love it and with his best friend there, Kyle will be in heaven."

"Sure, bring them along. The more the merrier."

Three days later Aliyah drove behind the SUV carrying Lauren, her husband, their two youngest sons and Kyle on the ten-minute drive to Paradise Cove. Since hearing he'd have a chance to ride a pony and catch a fish, her son had been bouncing off the walls. It felt good to see him happy. It also reminded her of how little time she had to spend with him these days. Lauren was like family and her boys were like his brothers, so she felt blessed to have them close by. But he was growing so fast. She felt bad for him, but worse for herself for missing precious moments in his life.

Once they'd reached Paradise Cove and taken the lake exit, she called Terrell.

"Hey, baby. Are you here?" he asked.

"Just took the lake exit."

"Then you're less than ten minutes away. Just follow the signs."

"Where should I meet you?"

"Once you've parked, walk back toward the parking entrance and cross the street. All the activities are here, around the lake. To the right of the lake are three large bouncy houses. Do you know what those are?"

"He asks the mother of a five-year-old."

"Hey, I'm proud of myself for being able to describe them because I just found out. Anyway, come to the big yellow one. I'll be waiting for you."

Fifteen minutes later, Terrell turned in her direction at the exact same time she spotted him. He waved them over.

"Mr. Drake!"

Terrell gave Kyle a fist bump. "Hello there, Kyle."

"I'm not Kyle. I'm an Avenger!"

Terrell glanced over at Aliyah. She shrugged and smiled with a look that conveyed the message: you're on your own.

"Why, of course. I knew that."

"Which one am I?"

"Oh, so there's more than one."

Aliyah chuckled. Terrell frowned.

"Yes, Mr. Drake!" Kyle crossed his arms. "Gosh, I thought you were cool!"

"I thought I was, too, Kyle, but—"

"Where's Mr. Adams? He knows all the Avenger names."

"I don't know but he's here, along with other Avengers, probably, otherwise known as your friends."

"Mommy, can I go find them?"

"We'll look for them in a minute, honey." She turned to Terrell. "Hello there."

Terrell held out his hand. "Ms. Robinson."

She accepted his handshake.

A simple, appropriate action except for the tone of his voice, the look in his eyes and how his fingers trailed against her palm ever so slightly. All while maintaining a friendly expression as though nothing was going on. A man shouldn't be able to make a handshake X-rated, but Terrell was about to moisten her panties.

It was all she could do not to jerk back her hand. Instead she pulled and at the same time turned to the people who'd joined her.

"Terrell, these are my friends. This is Lauren, her husband, Calvin, and her sons, Cody and Conner, who attend the center."

"I thought I recognized you," Terrell said, shaking the hand of the ten-year-old. While shaking Conner's hand, he spoke to Kyle. "This is your friend from school."

"And home, and everything! He's an Avenger, too!"

Terrell laughed. "I've seen you two playing together.

It's good to meet all of you. Let me give you a quick lay of the land."

With that, a raucous afternoon of fun, rides, laughter and carnival-style junk food began. Aliyah was relieved to see so many from the center. That she was there, seen with Terrell, did not stand out. At various times the parties split, with the children going one way, accompanied by one of the center's interns, and the couples enjoying some alone time. It was during one such time that Aliyah found herself meeting some of Terrell's family, thereby breaking the rule to not do it.

They'd just left a target game where Terrell won her a large stuffed bear when an attractive, familiar-looking couple approached them.

"I see someone's enjoying the festivities," the woman said to him, before addressing Aliyah with an outstretched hand. "Hi, I'm Teresa. The good twin."

Terrell feigned offense as the ladies shook hands. "Atka, did you not school your wife on how to behave in public?"

"No," the handsome man answered. "She skipped my class."

Everyone laughed.

"Sis, this is my friend Aliyah Robinson. Aliyah, my baby sister, Teresa, and her husband, Atka."

"It's nice meeting you both. Now I know why you looked so familiar," she said to Teresa. "You two really look alike."

"It's why I'm in therapy," Teresa said, deadpan.

"Best thing that ever happened to her," Terrell quickly responded. Through this it was clear to see that the love between these two knew no bounds.

"Where's everybody?" Terrell asked Teresa.

"Let's see. Monique and a few others are over at Warren and Charlie's. Ike and Audrey were playing hosts to some power couple from DC. Niko's busy being mayor. I saw Mom and Dad earlier but I think they left. That leaves all the fun to us."

Aliyah enjoyed all the event had to offer: food, fun, games and seeing her little man giddy with excitement. And sugar. At one point, she let Kyle go with the Hensleys to enjoy rides with Conner and visit the haunted house. Terrell took this opportunity to whisk her away, a few miles farther down the road, to the home of Warren, the grape-growing rancher, and his wife, Charlie, who with her jean shorts, tank top, cowboy hat and boots was the epitome of a 21st-century cowgirl. Had she roped a steer or rode a bucking bronco, Aliyah would not have been surprised. Nice enough, though. And down-to-earth, despite a home that seemed plucked from an interior design magazine, surrounded by land that was postcard perfect. As they left, Terrell drove her by Warren's neighbors, Teresa and Atka, who'd built a home for their many trips back to PC from Alaska, Atka's home state and place of their main residence.

Back at the festival, she met Ike and his date, watched Niko in action and quickly saw why he'd garnered the vote. Though each wielded it differently, every Drake man she'd met had an indefinable quality that was easy to notice and hard to resist. His brief yet passionate speech about the town's bright future made her want to cheer and she didn't even live there.

A fireworks display timed to music was the exclamation point to a perfect holiday. Five minutes after the last Roman candle boom, Kyle was asleep in Terrell's arms.

"We can take him with us," Lauren offered, as they all walked to the parking lot.

"That's okay. I'm heading home, too."

Terrell and Aliyah continued to her car. After Terrell placed Kyle in the car seat, Aliyah made sure he was strapped in securely.

"Thank you for inviting us here," she said, turning to face Terrell. "I couldn't have imagined how much fun this would be. I've never seen Kyle so happy."

Terrell reached out to hold her but she stepped back. "Too many eyes," she explained. "And as it is, I might have to make a stop at UC Davis to remove all the daggers the Tee Drake groupies were shooting at my back."

"Couldn't have been more than I should have thrown at all the men checking you out. But I wasn't worried. They got to look, but I get to touch. So what are we doing?"

"I'm going home."

"Why don't you come over to my house? It's just going to be my fam, a few friends."

"Because I have a son who needs to be put to bed."

"We've got beds at our house."

"Yes, but I'm going to put him in the one in his room."

He opened her car door. She climbed inside. "Then you know what's getting ready to happen, right?"

After starting the car, she looked up at him. "What?"

"I'm going to be in the one in your room. Text me your address." He turned and walked away.

"Terrell!" she yelled softly, if there was such a thing, so as not to wake the little one. She thought about simply not sending her address. That was an easy enough solution to not doing what she said she'd never do, and break another rule.

Except one should never say never. And that the prerogative of a woman to change her mind was a well-known fact. And it had been a long time since San Francisco.

So she texted him her address, and hurried home to welcome her guest.

Chapter 11

Once home, Aliyah lay Kyle on top of his bedcovers and took a quick shower. After spritzing her body with an organic concoction of vanilla and jasmine oils diluted in distilled water, she brushed back her hair, wrapped her body in a satiny, flowered kimono and returned to Kyle's room. She'd barely managed to remove the costume from her sleeping Avenger and tuck him into bed before her message indicator vibrated.

"That can't be Terrell," she mumbled, looking at her watch as she crossed over to her room and the nightstand where her phone lay.

There's a special delivery at your door. Come open it.

She did, and was immediately enveloped in a bear hug followed by a kiss so long and deep it threatened her breathing.

"Wait," she panted, finally breaking away, a hand to her chest as she stepped around him to close the door.

"You all right, babe?"

She put a finger to her mouth and used the other to direct him toward her bedroom. Once there, and with her door firmly shut, she took a deep breath. "Kyle's a pretty sound sleeper but I don't want to chance him hearing you.

That Mr. Drake came to visit Mommy is a story I don't want spread."

"I can understand that."

"To answer your question, yes, I'm all right. Though that was some kiss. It almost left me short of breath."

"Baby, that's what I'm here for. To take your breath away."

"Oh, Lord. Is that what's his name making a come-back? Silky?"

"Which family member opened their big mouth?"

"My lips are sealed."

"It had to be Teresa. I'm going to get her for that."

Aliyah watched Terrell unbutton and remove his shirt, then sit on her bed and begin unlacing his sneakers. She joined him on the bed. "By all means, make yourself comfortable."

"Oh, I'm going to do more than that." He stood, then unzipped and removed his pants.

She rested back on her haunches, her eyes lowered to half-mast. "Just what are you going to do, Mr. Drake?"

He lowered his voice even more. "I'm going to get rid of any and all obstructions between us." He pulled down and stepped out of his underwear. His dick—thick, long, hard, ready—sprang up like a cobra ready to strike.

He placed a knee on the bed, reached for the kimono belt and loosened the knot. "Like this." His eyes never left hers as he pushed the fabric away from her body, leaving her exposed, wanting. He ran a finger down the side of her face, continuing to her chest and over to flick a nipple.

Fully on the bed now, he lowered his head. "Then," he whispered, his breath flowing across her nipple now pebbled with lust, "I'm going to kiss." His lips caressed her skin. "Lick." His tongue—slow, wet—laved across one nipple, then the other, trailed to her stomach and around her inward navel. Lower, to the triangular paradise now moist with desire, her pearl plump and exposed, ripe for the plucking…and he did, with relish. He nipped with his teeth and lapped with his tongue, parting her folds and lavishing her with all of the desire he'd held at bay all day.

He spread her legs wider, pushed his tongue deeper, branding her spot with the precision of a tattoo artist, and just as lasting.

"Mmm, baby, you taste so good."

And on and on he went, licking, laving, lapping, loving, lower and lower still.

To a part of her body that no man had ever touched.

"Ooh, Terrell…"

"What? You don't like it?"

"No. I mean, I don't know. I've never—" She gasped, words lost to this foreign, excruciatingly maddening touch of his tongue. Hot. Wet. Licking her there.

He guided her over, onto her stomach. Her body quivered, goose bumps appearing at the heat of his gaze. His dick, already swollen, became even more engorged.

"This right here," he whispered softly, almost reverently, as he squeezed her cheeks apart. And together. And apart again. "This is my favorite part of your body." He kissed it. "Perfect." He kissed it again. "The best I've ever seen."

He ran a finger down each crease. Back and forth. Making her wetter with each long swipe. "Damn, you're so wet for me. So instead of telling you what's about to happen… I'll show you."

He turned her over, grabbed her thighs, buried his head in her sweet spot and thrust his tongue in deep.

Aliyah yelped, the sudden delicious invasion making her come with abandon. She grabbed a pillow to absorb the screams as on the waves of the seismic orgasm he positioned himself over her and sheathed himself inside her tight core. For minutes, or was it hours, he moved inside her, taking her over the top once again. Still hard, still hungry, he flipped them over. Laced his hands behind his head and watched her slide down his shaft, her breasts swaying in time with her hips, her eyes fluttering closed at the hypnotic feel of him inside her. Later, bodies glistening with sweat, tendrils of hair clinging against her neck and back, she rode with him once again over the edge. His groan deep and powerful, her body completely spent.

Collapsing on top of him she had breath enough left for only one word. "Amazing."

It was a little after midnight. They lay naked, spooning, in her queen-size bed.

"You're dangerous."

Terrell pulled her tighter, nudged her with his package. "How so?"

She gave him a look. "You have to ask?"

"I'd never assume anything."

"I now understand why you have such a large…female following." He laughed. She joined him. "Not the comment you expected?"

"It's why I don't assume. But don't think everybody gets what you got tonight. That was special. Just for you."

She eyed him again. "Really?"

He turned on his side, the gaze meeting hers that of a very satisfied man. "Yes, really. You've got me feeling you on a deep level. For real."

She looked away from him. "Don't get mad at your sister. The nickname fits."

"So it was Teresa. I knew it."

"Says that it's what makes you such a successful businessman. Can sell honey to bees she told me. A gift of gab that is as smooth as silk."

"She said all that?"

"No, I added the last part."

"My spiels work because they are honest, and come

from the heart. When I say something, I mean it. Besides, for you I'd rather be thought of as silky for other, more personal uses of my mouth and tongue."

Aliyah took a deep breath and tried to slow the heartbeat that his words had increased. Not to mention how her pussy just quivered. This conversation was getting into scary territory. And her feelings were following suit. "You've got me breaking rules, dude! Rule one, no serious anything."

"Oh, so this is serious now?" he said, chuckling.

"No! But meeting your family makes it feel serious." She turned her head toward him even though the room was dark. "Have you ever met the parents of a booty call?"

"I'm more than a booty call."

"No, you're not." His confident, disbelieving laugh was slightly infuriating. "You're a friend with benefits."

"If you say so."

"Rule two," she continued, ignoring his smugness. "No male sleepovers, except for Kyle's friends."

"No worries. I'll make sure we stay awake all night."

This earned a swat on his exposed thigh. "No, you won't. I have to work tomorrow."

"What time do you have to be there?"

"Not until noon," she answered with a grateful sigh. "But don't expect pancakes for breakfast. You'll be leaving shortly."

"You're putting me out?"

"Yes."

"What, it's screw and through?"

"Absolutely."

"Ha!"

"Shh! Quiet, before you wake Kyle, and I have to explain what Mr. Drake is doing in Mommy's bed."

He turned, and settled on his back. "Aliyah."

"Hmm?"

"Is that the real reason you were so against meeting

my family, because to do so would change your views of our relationship?"

"It's not a—"

"Okay, friendship. My bad."

A second passed, and then another.

"No, not really."

"What's the reason?"

Aliyah repositioned herself to lie on her back, too. "Because being around families like yours reminds me of Ernest's family, Kyle's father. As I've already shared, that was not a good experience."

"Made worse because your ex did not stand by your side."

"That hurt the most, but it wasn't the only thing."

"Explain that."

She let out a sigh. "It's not important."

"It is to me."

"Why?"

He reached out in the darkness, ran a gentle finger down the side of her face, and down her arm, before resting it on her hip. "Because I like you, Aliyah Robinson. And I'm trying to get to know the person beneath the scrubs, and the tough, screw-and-through exterior. That's all."

Several seconds passed, to the point where Terrell doubted she'd answer. But she did.

"Being around Ernest's family often left me feeling insignificant. Not just because they were wealthy, not just the materialism. It was also their societal recognition, their knowledge of a family lineage they could take back generations and their amazing ability to simply ignore that which they did not believe in or think important. Huge matters, like world hunger, or global warming, or race relations or an economy spiraling out of control. Situations that sometimes impacted me and my family. It was as though if they didn't talk about it, it didn't exist.

"The Westcotts are native Rhode Islanders whose fore-fathers were prominent members of the larger community since, if they are to be believed, the ink began to dry on the Emancipation Proclamation. His father, a lawyer, has been a councilman for years. His mother is a socialite." Said as though cotton were stuffed up her nose and elic-iting the laughter she intended. "Their daughter, Jane, is married to a banker, whose Boston-based family is also part of the elite. So Ernest holding a conversation with me, much less dating and, gasp and sputter, getting me preg-nant, was akin to murder in the first degree."

"How'd you meet him?"

"At Brown University. He was a senior. I was a fresh-man minding my own business when he stopped my stroll across the campus and asked me on a date."

"That just goes to show you how fine you are because many of those brothers don't socialize outside their circle."

"I don't think he had plans for me beyond the sheets. My intelligence surprised him."

"A woman with a booty and a brain!"

"You're silly. One date turned into several and before you know it, we were official. After six months or so, he invited me to a dance. Big mistake. One look at me and his parents knew I wasn't upper crust. I think he'd hoped my becoming a doctor would get me a pass, but no. His mother was not having it. She didn't like me and made no attempt to hide it. His father was friendlier. His sister, cor-dial enough. Shortly after this, I got pregnant. Totally un-expected. Was on the pill and everything. Thought about not having it. That was a really tough time."

"Why did you?" Terrell asked, with a comforting squeeze.

"I loved Ernest, and wanted to be with him. Yes, the baby presented a huge challenge, but I thought that to-gether, we could get through it. He did, too. Until the ultimatum, when he was told to break off all contact with me or else. I think a part of him wanted to break out of the roles he'd been handed by his parents, to live a life that was driven more by the heart than the head and what's considered socially acceptable. I think a part of him really loved me. But that wasn't enough to risk defying his parents and losing a hefty inheritance. By the time the you-know-what hit the fan I was four months along and out of options."

"You've had to be strong."

"Yes."

She turned and laid her head on Terrell's shoulder. He wrapped an arm around her. "How did you feel around my family today?"

"I felt fine. They all treated me nicely, didn't act too uppity."

"What do you mean, 'too'?"

She laughed. "Hey, don't get offended. Like it or not you're part of the upper class. There's an aura about people like you, whether or not you intend it. Not with you so much, but your brother Ike? Definitely. And that woman he was with? She could party in Rhode Island and fit right in."

"I'll admit Audrey is a trip, especially around another beautiful woman. She's frustrated because after dating Ike off and on for a decade, my brother still hasn't proposed."

"Warren and Charlie? They were nice. And your twin, Teresa, and her husband...what's his name?"

"Atka."

"Yeah, him. They're high-end. He was quiet, but your twin went out of her way to include me in the conversation. I appreciated that."

"Aliyah."

"Yes, Terrell."

"My last name is Drake, not Westcott. Yes, my family

is wealthy but we're not stuck up. They will adore you as much as I do and will never, ever make you feel less than the beautiful woman you are. Are you listening?"

"Yes, I hear you."

"Good. So drop the cape and lose the heart shield. You don't have to be tough with me."

She reached up and kissed his cheek, then settled against his shoulder. "Thank you. But I'm keeping my cape."

"I guess that's okay. Might need your help in beating the women off me."

"Whatever, you cocky dude."

"I thought that's what you loved about me."

This earned him another swat, on the arm this time.

"I've heard about your jerk of an ex's family. Now, tell me about yours."

"What do you want to know?"

"Whatever you want to tell me—siblings, parents, growing up in New York."

"When people hear New York, they think of Manhattan. I grew up in Brooklyn. There's a difference. Each borough has its own personality."

"I look forward to a personal tour."

"That could be arranged."

"So tell me about it."

"I loved growing up there. Sure, it was hard. Times were tough. My parents didn't always get along. We siblings fought like…siblings. But love was there, always, and unconditional acceptance. The whole block was like one big family. There was a unique, palpable energy created by all the cultures and classes and languages, dialects, foods, traditions…all blending together. When I was little, the block was one big playground. We'd hopscotch, double-dutch and play games in the middle of the street, to an international soundtrack. From hip-hop to R and B, reggae to calypso, the straight-ahead jazz from our neighbor, Mr. Johnny, to the gospel every Sunday by Miss Francine. It was the best life, fun and carefree.

"By the time I turned twelve the area had started to change. Gangs, drugs and illegal activities that used to be on the periphery made their way to our neighborhood, and our block. When the neighborhood changed, some of the neighbors changed. Some of my friends changed. Mama tightened the reins and I lost my innocent outlook. I'm the oldest of five, three brothers and another sister, and felt I had to protect them. I still do."

"The dark side can come off looking quite attractive. How'd you keep from getting caught up?"

"My parents. Mama is a nurse, with a strong work ethic. My father is a jack of all trades—construction, handyman, repairman, moving man, whatever you need. He used to drive the train—the subway—until he got injured and had to go on disability. He received a small settlement that they set aside as a college fund for us. The odd jobs keep him busy and contributing to the household.

"They both taught education as the holy grail, the ticket to a better life. I had observant teachers who encouraged me and when they saw that their lessons were too easy, they pushed me higher, farther, faster. I developed a love for learning so while my friends were into boys, I was into books."

"Really."

"Uh-huh."

They talked well into the night. She was impressed at Terrell's genuine interest in her, asking questions and listening intently. It hadn't been this way with the others. Most conversations had been all about them. By the time they spooned into peaceful slumber, there was something else Aliyah was really into. The man beside her.

* * *

"Mommy?"

"Yes, Kyle."

"I had a dream last night."

"Sit down and eat your cereal, Kyle." She poured almond milk into her bowl and joined him at the table. "What did you dream about?"

"Mr. Drake."

Aliyah almost choked on granola. "Oh, uh, really?" she sputtered, taking a sip of water to clear her throat.

Kyle nodded. "I heard his voice. He called you baby!"

"Hmm. That was some dream." What had this child been doing awake at three in the morning?

"I woke up because I thought it was real!"

How'd he hear us? Then she remembered. Terrell had called out to her as she left to get water. Now, because of his slip-up, she was on a slippery slope. The very reason why she had rules in the first place. "Dreams can often seem real, honey, even though they're make-believe."

"Hey, maybe we can invite Mr. Drake over!"

Lord, this child! "Why would we do that, honey?"

"So we can play together!"

Been there. Done that. That's why she was dragging right now.

"Mr. Drake is a grown man, Kyle. You'll have to play with boys your own age."

"But he played with me on Halloween.."

"That was different. Lots of kids from your class were there."

"Then I could show him my puzzles and stuff because he teaches math!"

"What about Mr. Adams? Don't you get to work with him and show him stuff in class?"

"Yes. But I like Mr. Drake. He's fun."

Aliyah wasn't sure how to feel about how much her son

liked Terrell. That he now had role models like Terrell and Luther was good. But she didn't want him becoming too attached. Herself, either, for that matter.

"Did you make your bed?" Another nod. "Then hurry and finish your sandwich. Miss Lauren will be here soon to pick you up."

Chapter 12

On Wednesday, Terrell wasn't scheduled to be at the center but he stopped by anyway.

"What's up, Big Lou!"

Luther walked over and offered a fist bump. "What are you doing here today?"

"Just stopped through real quick—checking on things. How's it going?"

"It's good, Tee. Great time with the family on the weekend. That thing y'all had at Drake Lake and the ranch? That was cool, man. My kids, the wife, everyone loved it."

"I can't take credit for any of that. There was a committee that put all of that together, the rides, everything. Wasn't even my land. That ranch belongs to Warren."

Luther waved off the comment. "Please, if it belongs to one Drake it belongs to all."

"True that." Terrell walked around the room. "You're doing a good job with these kids, man. I never could have imagined it, but daddyhood looks good on you."

"There's nothing like it, Tee. You should give it a try."

Terrell raised his hands in surrender. "That's all right. I'm good."

Luther laughed. "Hey, I'm glad you stopped by. Check this out." He walked over to a bookshelf filled with colorful books, puzzles and stuffed animals, and reached for a piece of paper on top of it.

"Look at this."

Terrell took the paper. It was filled with mathematical equations. Aside from the fact that it looked to have been written by one of Luther's charges, it looked like good old addition and subtraction to him. He shrugged. "What about it?"

"Kyle did that."

"Did what? Copied this out of a workbook?"

"No. He did the math."

Terrell looked at the paper again. These weren't a string of "two plus two" or "five plus five." The first problem involved three figures. The second, four. By the end of the page, the problems were in the hundreds of thousands to either be added or subtracted.

Terrell looked at Luther. "Impressive. But I guess not too terribly surprising considering his mother is a doctor. He's probably been playing with her calculator since he could crawl."

"You misunderstand, my brother. The kid did this without a calculator, without using his fingers and without taking much time to give the answer. I was the one who used a calculator to see if what he wrote down was correct!"

"Are you kidding me?"

"Man, I swear. Blew my mind. I said to myself, we've got a little genius in the class."

"You mind if I take this with me? I want to make sure his mother knows about it."

"Well, actually, I was going to tell her myself. Give me an excuse to, you know, have a conversation with her fine behind."

Terrell folded the paper and placed it in his shirt pocket, talking over his shoulder as he walked to the door. "Go home and converse with your lady. I'll make sure Ms. Robinson gets the news about her son."

After a quick visit with Marva and an impromptu meeting with the center's director, Terrell headed back to Drake Realty. On the way, he called Aliyah.

"Hey."

"Hello, beautiful. How are you?" he asked.

"Busy. What's up?"

"Called to tell you about your son."

"What, did something happen?"

"No. He's fine."

"Oh, okay. Then what?"

"Your son might be a little genius. Have you had him tested?"

"No."

"You should. Luther showed me some math problems he did. I was blown away."

"He has a thing for numbers."

"I'll say. Some of my teenagers couldn't handle the problems he solved."

"Look, I gotta go."

"But you know about this, right? His ability to calculate in his head and stuff?"

"Not really. Tell me later. 'Bye."

Later that evening, his call went to voice mail. She didn't return it.

The next day he arrived early at the center, before it was time to tutor his students. He wanted to see Kyle's ability for himself. He peeked into the room. It was empty. He walked outside to the playground behind the center. Luther sat on a low wall watching the students periodically, and checking his cell phone.

"Good afternoon, Luther."

"Hey, Terrell. What's up, man?"

"Not a lot—waiting for my guys to get here."

"How's it going with them?"

"Hits and misses. Improvement overall, and a few who've grown significantly. But there are a couple who just aren't interested in learning. I'll be fortunate to talk them out of not quitting school altogether."

"That's the way it is sometimes. We do what we can where we can."

"It's crazy how a kid as young as Kyle can run mathematical rings around kids more than twice his age."

"Yeah, I told the wife about what I saw him do yesterday. She found it hard to believe he'd done it on his own."

"I do, too, to be honest with you."

"You should check it out. Hey, Kyle!"

Kyle was sitting at the edge of the asphalt, playing with rocks. When Luther called, he jumped up and ran over.

"Hi, Mr. Drake!"

"Hey there, Kyle. How are you, buddy?"

"Good."

"So I hear. Yesterday, Mr. Adams showed me the math problems you solved. All of the answers were correct. That was very good, Kyle."

"Thank you."

"Mr. Drake would like to see you work. Do you think you could solve a few problems for him?" Luther asked. Kyle nodded.

"Good." Luther looked at Terrell. "You want to do it as soon as this break is over?"

"I'd rather do it now, without the other kids. Hold on." Terrell reached for his phone and called the center's office. "Miss Marva, can you ask one of the interns to come to the playground? I need someone to watch Luther's class for a bit." He paused to listen. "Good, thanks."

A few minutes later, one of the interns came outside. Terrell, Luther and Kyle went back to Luther's classroom. Terrell wrote a six-figure mathematical problem on a whiteboard and asked Kyle to solve it. After a few seconds, Kyle walked over and wrote down the answer.

Terrell looked at Luther, who shrugged. "Told you."

He felt a bit embarrassed, but Terrell pulled out his phone, tapped the calculator app and checked Kyle's answer.

"That's correct, Kyle," he said.

"I know." Said without a shred of doubt or ego.

"How'd you figure it out so fast?"

"I don't know, Mr. Drake. I just do it."

"Here, let me give you another one." Terrell placed another problem on the board. Kyle solved it just as quickly. He looked at Luther. "To actually see him do it is even more amazing."

"He's not counting on his fingers or taking a lot of time to think about it."

Terrell pulled out his phone. "I'm going to put three problems on the board this time, okay, little man?"

"Okay." Said in a tone that implied he was totally bored. "Then can I go back outside?"

Luther looked at his watch. "It's time for them to come back in. I'll go get them."

Terrell finished the problems, handed Kyle the marker, then pulled out his phone and took a video of Kyle as he quickly solved the problems. After confirming that once again, the answers were accurate, he gave Kyle a high five.

"No wonder you were so interested in the flash cards I had a few weeks ago. You might be ready to study with the big boys after all!"

"The teenagers?" Kyle's eyes widened.

"Yes. Would you like that?"

"I don't know."

Terrell noted the boy's discomfort and belatedly realized the prospect of being called out in a room full of teens may sound intimidating. "No worries. We'll leave you here for now, okay?"

"Yes, that's better. Thank you, Mr. Drake."

"Thank you for showing me your skills."

Luther returned with the rest of the kids and Terrell left to tutor his teens. On the way he attached the video of Kyle's performance to a text for Aliyah. The question was simple: Like mother, like son?

Chapter 13

Aliyah stifled a yawn as she stepped into the break room. Her cranky exhaustion was all Terrell's fault. That walking caramel lollipop had strolled into her world and turned it upside down. Booty call. Yeah, right. That's what she called him but they both knew he was becoming more than that. Much more. But she wasn't ready to admit it. Nor was she willing to stop it from happening.

After finding an empty table and sitting down with salad and caffeine-laced soda in hand, she pulled out her cell phone and took it out of silent mode. Seeing Terrell's name reminded her of their quick conversation earlier today. She opened his text message and smiled at his question. Until she read it again. Then it became a reminder. Like mother, like son. Though it is a statistic she'd never wanted to be a part of, she was a single mother raising a son. Even now, at the age of five, her son was very aware that unlike his friend Conner, Kyle's daddy was not in the home. Thankfully, aside from his number fascination, Kyle's attention span was short. The few times he'd asked about his father, her honest yet brief answers had been enough.

"Where is my daddy?"

"Your father lives in Rhode Island."

"Where is that?"

"It is near where Nana lives in New York."

"Why doesn't he live with us?"

"Because he is married to someone else."

An image of Terrell popped into her head. She shut down the train of thought before it could catch hold. She was not one to fantasize about what could never be. She had no doubt that someday Terrell would make a great father. But it wouldn't be to Kyle.

She opened the attachment and watched the video. Confused, she played it again, watched as her son walked over to the board, glanced at the numbers, then quickly wrote down the answer. He did the same thing with the next problem, and the next. It was clear he'd either memorized the answer or was copying it from what she couldn't see. She called Terrell.

"How'd you do it?"

"You watched the video."

"Yes."

"I didn't do anything. It was all Kyle."

"Look, Terrell. I know my son. He's been hooked on math games and puzzles since he was three, but he didn't solve those problems. Did you have him memorize the numbers or were they written somewhere out of camera range?"

"Neither. I came up with the problems in my head and wrote them down. He solved them."

"That quickly?"

"Yep."

"I don't believe you."

"I didn't believe Luther when he told me, either. Told him I had to see it to believe it. I saw. I believe."

"But how? It's like he just glanced at the numbers and then wrote down the answer."

"That's exactly what happened. That's why I called you all excited, woman! But you blew me off. You were busy."

"I didn't and I was. Wow. He stands there for just a second, then walks up to the board and writes the answer left to right. How is he adding those numbers?"

"I pretty much asked him the same question, asked how he knew the answers. He said he just did."

"Maybe Lauren's been teaching him. Or Conner's oldest brother, Conrad. He's around fifteen or so. Maybe he's been working with him."

Her voice trailed off as she watched the short video once again.

"I think it's him taking after his brilliant mommy." No answer. "Aliyah."

"Sorry. I'm sending the video to Lauren, and asking if she or Conrad have been working with him." She also sent it to her family. "Now, what did you say?"

Terrell repeated his statement.

"Thank you, but Mommy wasn't solving problems like that at five years old. Darn it."

"What?"

"Mama has a dinosaur phone. It says the file is too big to send her."

"Upload it to YouTube. That way you can just send the link."

"Good idea." She looked at her watch. Break time was over. She walked toward the nurses' station. "I'll do it when I get home."

"Cool. Send me the link, too."

"Okay."

"Are you rushing me off the phone again?"

"Pretty much."

"Ha! You're a trip."

"No, I'm east coast. We keep it real. Your workday is over but I'm still on the clock."

"What do you say I meet you when you get off the clock?"

"Negative. When I finally get to bed, the only thing I want to do is sleep."

"That's unfortunate."

"I'll let you make it up to me."

"When?"

"Friday night. We can go somewhere and be naughty for a couple hours."

"Negative. Friday's too far away."

"It's tomorrow, Terrell."

"Exactly. And I haven't seen you since—"

"Two nights ago."

"That long?"

"Goodbye, Terrell."

"Call me later."

"Okay."

Later, when a surgery had to be rescheduled, Aliyah found herself with an hour of downtime. She updated a couple of patient files and then tackled the process of uploading her son's video to YouTube. A few minutes later, she had a link. She resent the text to her family, sent the link to Lauren and Terrell and finished her shift.

On her way to the car, she pulled out her phone.

Four missed calls. Eight missed text messages. Her heart leaped into her throat. What had happened to Kyle?

Then she remembered. The video. She reached her car, got in and tapped the first message. It was from her twenty-two-year-old brother, Kieran, who'd recently graduated from NYU.

Wow, sis. That was pretty cool. Now tell me how you got Kyle to remember all those answers, cause no five-year-old can do all that.

Next text. Her twenty-year-old brother, Joseph, who was attending a college in Iowa on a full, four-year basketball scholarship.

Look at little shorty, taking after his uncle! This is impressive. If it's not fake.

Text number three, from a cousin in Atlanta. The video had already reached extended family. Her mother, Aliyah reckoned. But still, that was fast.

Is this my cuzzo??? Wow!!! He's so smart, but then again, look at his mama. Xoxo

The last text was from Terrell.

Hope you don't mind that I sent your son's video link to a few people. No one can believe it. At least half of them have responded back to ask me how I got him to memorize those numbers! LOL. Your son is really gifted, A. You should probably have him tested. He's probably a genius. Like you...

His words warmed her heart, and other places. Handsome, successful, unassuming and genuinely a nice guy. She'd noticed it at the Halloween festivities. A smile here, a compliment there, everyone happy to see him because he made people feel good. No wonder he was a chick magnet. Good thing their relationship was casual and she didn't care about what monkeys were in his circus. Let someone else be the ringleader. Yes. That sounded good. She tapped the missed-calls icon and saw that most were from family, though Terrell had called as well. After activating her car's hands-free system, she pulled out of the parking lot and returned his call.

"Good evening."

Two common words. But the way he said them, slow and easy, in that deep, slightly raspy voice, with her imagining how his lips moved and his tongue rolled, caused her to almost bypass the next corner, where she was to make a left and continue to the highway, and Paradise Cove.

"Hello."

"Baby, I'm concerned. You sound exhausted."

"By Thursday night, I'm pretty beat. But having Friday morning off gives me time to get rejuvenated."

"Your hard work is going to pay off."

"Let us pray."

"You're headed home?"

"Yes, and no."

"What does that mean?"

"Yes I'm headed home and no, you can't come over."

"Did I ask to come over?"

"You did earlier. I made an exception to my rule the other night but don't want you to get used to coming to my house. As the video you shot plainly shows, Kyle is a very bright kid. He heard you the other night and thought it was a dream. If he saw you, we'd have a whole bunch of explaining to do."

"He said that?" She nodded. "I'm sorry. Teresa wants to talk to you about how smart Kyle is."

"Who?'

"Really? My twin?"

"Excuse me but I only met her once. And on a day where I met about a dozen other people."

"You're excused."

"I don't know what I'd tell her. The games and apps I've downloaded for him are nowhere near as complicated as the problems he solved. Lauren said she's never taught him anything like that and doesn't think her son has, either." The last few words were mumbled through a yawn.

"How far are you from your house?"

"Not far, why?"

"Because you're yawning, and I don't want to worry about you falling asleep at the wheel."

"I won't. I'm almost at Lauren's to pick up Kyle. In twenty minutes, I'll be in bed."

"Hey, I've got an idea."

"What?"

"Do you think Lauren could watch Kyle for a little while longer?"

"She could, but she won't because I'm here to pick him up."

"Babe, I can't explain now but can you trust me? Can you ask her to watch him, and then be ready to leave your house in an hour?"

"Leave my house in an hour?!"

"Okay, thirty minutes?"

"No, Terrell."

Terrell groaned. "Man, that same stubborn drive that makes you so successful is driving me crazy right now."

"Then I'll solve that by letting you go."

"That's fine. But I'm stubborn, too. So ask Lauren to watch Kyle, please, and be ready in half an hour."

"Wait, Terrell, don't—"

But he had. The line was dead.

Aaliyah pulled into the Hensley driveway, but kept her car idling. It had been a long time since a man told her what to do. Aside from her father, it had never happened, come to think of it. So why start now? She turned off the car and opened the door. But curiosity stopped her. What was Terrell up to? Where did he want her to go? The last time she'd trusted him, they'd ended up spending a magical night in San Francisco. Hmm. She closed the door and called Lauren. A die-hard romantic, Lauren had sided with Terrell and practically threatened her with bodily harm if she came in to get her son. So she didn't. She drove home.

Thirty minutes went by. Nothing happened.

Forty minutes. She texted Terrell. What's up? No answer.

An hour. Aliyah took off her clothes and got into bed.

Fifteen minutes later, she heard her indicator chirp. Terrell.

You ready?

The nerve of this guy! She yanked up her phone. No. I'm in bed. Asleep. She placed the phone on the nightstand and pulled up the covers. *Chirp*. She tried to ignore it. Couldn't. Grabbed the phone again.

Go look out your living room window.

She resent her last message, and hoped this time that not only would his phone get it, but that he would, too. *Chirp*.

It was now obvious to Aliyah that he was not getting her message. But he would. She turned off her ringer.

Five minutes went by…before someone rang her doorbell.

"What the heck?" She sprang out of bed, ready to give Terrell a piece of her mind. *So this is why he wanted Kyle gone? So he could come over here against my wishes?*

She reached the door, yanked it open and…looked into the face of a startled, uniformed stranger. Really should have checked that peephole. But she was thankful for the screen door, which she promptly locked.

"Why are you at my door?"

"Forgive me, Ms. Robinson. I didn't mean to startle you. I am here at the request of Mr. Drake. He says he could not reach you by phone, and asked that I let you know your limo is waiting."

"My limo?" The stranger stepped back, allowing her to see a big, black, shiny limousine fairly glistening under the streetlight. Her jaw dropped.

She heard her cell phone ring. Her attention went from

the man to the sound of the phone and back. Her mind was too fuzzy with fatigue to think. "Just a minute," she told the driver and then rushed to get the phone.

"Hello?"

"Good, you answered. Is Ed there, with the limo?"

"You mean the stranger who scared me half to death ringing my doorbell?"

"Sorry, baby. Couldn't be helped. You didn't answer your phone so I told him to get you. Are you ready?"

Aliyah had never been so flummoxed in her life. Didn't she text this man that she was in bed and asleep? Twice? That she was neither right now was inconsequential.

Terrell continued, as if reading her mind. "I know you're tired. This will make you feel better. I promise. Will you trust me, throw something on and be nice to Ed as he brings you to your destination?"

"Which is?"

"A surprise. Are you coming?"

"Yes," she finally huffed.

"Good. I'll see you soon."

She hung up and all but stomped back into her bedroom and over to the closet. "I can't believe he's pulled this," she mumbled, pulling on jeans and replacing her night-shirt with a simple T-shirt. *I shouldn't go. I should just go out there, tell Mr. Ed that's there's been a mistake and send the limo on its merry way.* She thought this, even as she slipped on sandals, reached for her purse and headed toward the door.

Half of her was exasperated at the gall this man had. But the other half, the lower half specifically, was getting excited.

Chapter 14

Terrell had surfed the internet, looking for sites of local companies that could provide the service he wanted. No luck. So he resorted to the familiar and called up his go-to girl.

She answered immediately. "Tee, what's up?"

"Hey, Tee. You still in town?"

"No. Atka had a business meeting first thing this morning so we left last night. I thought I told you."

"You may have. There's a lot going on."

"Tell me about it."

"From what I saw, you're handling it well—marriage, motherhood, the blog and how fast it's growing. Sometimes I still can't believe I'm an uncle. Not once, but twice!"

"Yes, my son, Logan David, and Warren's daughter, Sage."

"Speaking of babies and baby making, where can I find a mobile spa company, someone who does manicures, pedicures, facials, et cetera, as a home visit?"

"Really, brother? All of that for a segue?"

"No," he said, laughing. "You know I'm always about family but my question is why I called."

"Is this for Aliyah?"

"Yes."

"Hmm. She's got you working, thinking outside the box. Normally it's your women doing all the work. Interesting.

Though I can see why. Not only is she gorgeous, but she's smart. And her son is the cutest. I like her."

"Good. Now can you help me?"

"Sure. When do you want to do it?"

"In about thirty minutes."

For anyone else such a request would have been impossible. But Teresa was one of the most connected women in all of PC, and the right amount of money could always get an appointment. So by the time he'd sent the limo and then texted Aliyah, everyone he'd summoned to take care of his lady was either setting up or on the way.

When she arrived, Terrell was waiting at the side door, the direct entrance to his wing of the Drake estate.

"Hello, beautiful." He gave her a hug.

Stepping back, she said, "This can't be your house."

"It belongs to my parents. This is just my wing. Come with me."

She took Terrell's outstretched hand and followed him down the hallway. "This is the largest private home I've ever seen," she whispered.

"It's pretty big," he said with a chuckle as they neared his suite. "Which is why you don't have to whisper. My parents are all the way on the other side and, trust me, you can holler even and they won't hear a thing."

"And we know this because... Never mind, don't answer that question." She took a moment to survey the pictures lining the hallway. "This is nice, Terrell. Really nice."

"Thank you."

"Did you grow up here?"

"Pretty much. My parents had this home built twenty years ago, when Golden Gates was established as the town's gated community. I had just turned eight when we moved in. My parents did a major renovation seven or eight years ago."

They reached his suite. The doors opened to a room that

had been transformed from a bedroom to a spa. Dim lighting combined with fragrant white candles to create an ambiance of fantasy. Aliyah was floored. "Did you do this?"

"I helped. Go on in."

She did, and was immediately drawn to his massive custom bed. "Wow, very nice. This room is fit for a king."

"And that—" he raised his arm in the other direction "—is for you, my queen."

She turned, and had to pick her jaw off the floor.

Amid the sea of flickering tea candles were two massage tables. A short distance from them, a spa pedicure chair. A delicious scent of jasmine mixed with something fruity tickled her nostrils. Soft music played in the background. Across the room, in the living area's fireplace, red embers glowed. Aliyah took in the fantastical scene and felt like Cinderella when invited to the ball.

Terrell came up behind her and placed his hands on her shoulders. She turned into his embrace. "This is all so amazing, Terrell. I don't know what to say."

"Then say nothing." He gave her a quick kiss on the lips. "Just enjoy."

She walked over to the massage table nearest her. "I was thinking about how badly I needed one of these just the other day! And this, with the music and the aromatherapy, is an even better atmosphere than I imagined. That's jasmine I smell, right?"

"Yes."

Aliyah turned, startled by the strange voice, even more surprised that there wasn't one person who'd quietly entered the room, but two.

"I'm sorry, dear friend. I did not mean to scare you."

"Aliyah, this is Sanje and Heaven, owners of Heavenly Spa Treatment, a mobile service that, as you can see, brings the spa to you."

"To further answer your question," the woman, Heaven,

said to Aliyah, "in the infuser is our product called Sur-render, a combination of jasmine, ylang-ylang, bergamot and a couple secret ingredients, all designed to help you de-stress, relax and be at peace."

"For me to achieve all of that may take more than just one sitting."

Terrell's voice turned sexy. "That can be arranged."

"We will travel wherever needed," Sanje said.

"Sounds great." Aliyah placed her hand on the table, felt the soft, cotton spread. "I'm ready."

Heaven stepped forward. "Then let's get started."

Thirty minutes in and Aliyah felt like putty in Heaven's capable hands. If his satisfied grunts were any indication, Sanje's work on Terrell was excellent as well. Aliyah luxu-riated in the feeling. She could get used to this. She could also get used to Terrell in her life. As quickly as the thought came, Aliyah worked to dispel it. She didn't know if she could trust someone like Terrell with her heart. But when it came to making that decision, she realized, it might be too late already.

Chapter 15

Terrell sauntered into the boardroom, more than ready for the Monday morning meeting at his family's firm. Since finding out that he was being considered for the position of VP of sales and marketing, he'd doubled his sales efforts, often working eighty-hour weeks. Last night he'd received an email that proved his efforts were paying off. A professional organization whose membership represented several companies planning expansion had chosen Drake Realty as their sole realtor and consulting firm.

"Good morning, all!" He continued to where the drinks were located.

"Morning, son." Ike, Sr. turned from pouring a cup of coffee to greet him.

The other ones present—Ike, Jr., Warren and the company directors—chimed in as well.

"Who's that kid everybody's talking about?" Ike, Jr. asked. "The math whiz who goes to our center."

"Where'd you see it?"

"Teresa's blog."

"She put it on her blog? Cool."

"I saw it last night. The little tyke is pretty popular. The video has already gotten over five thousand hits."

"Seriously?" Terrell pulled out his phone and clicked the YouTube icon. "Dang, that's crazy. The video's been up less than seventy-two hours."

The director of property management asked for the link, and checked it out. "Wow, that's really something. Are you sure you didn't coach this kid?"

Terrell shook his head. "Not at all. In fact, I should make another one where people give him arbitrary numbers off the top of their heads so people know we're not cheating."

"I say unless this young man is ready to sell some residential and commercial property, we table this discussion and get on to the Drake matters at hand."

"This is a Drake matter, Dad." Everyone looked at Terrell. "Whatever positive buzz is generated through this video is great for the Drake Community Center—its programs, activities, et cetera. It could bring national attention to not only the center, but also our town. Yes, the child is very bright. But it doesn't hurt us that he is being taught our center. Whether or not he'll opt for a career in real estate is a decision that is decades away. But that his video could benefit our center in the short term is a very real possibility."

"Good point, Terrell. So now that I have a more complete picture of this kid and the relevance of his video to various Drake holdings, can someone send me the link?"

Aliyah stared at the number in disbelief. An hour ago, Terrell had texted a message for her to pull up Kyle's video to see how many views it had gotten. A week ago, she was surprised to see that over five thousand people had watched her son solve math problems. When Terrell mentioned that his sister had posted the link on her blog, Aliyah believed it was her subscribers and the blog's growing popularity that had caused the spike in numbers. When texts from her brother said his video had gone viral, this number was what she thought he was talking about. But no. He'd seen what she was now looking at. A video with over a million views.

She called Lauren. "Hey, girl. Did you know that Kyle's video has gone viral?"

"No!" Aaliyah could tell Lauren was at her computer; could hear her clicking keys. "Oh, my goodness, Aaliyah, this is amazing! Your son makes being smart and doing math look fun!"

"Terrell suggested I have his IQ tested. I agree, and plan to look into it."

"Speaking of Terrell, how's it going?"

"How's what going?"

"Oh, right. It's just casual sex. Doesn't mean anything."

"Exactly."

"Though seeing the two of you together, that's not the vibe I got. You make a good couple. Even Calvin said so."

"We enjoy each other's company. I'm not thinking of anything beyond that."

"You know what? That's probably best. But getting back to Kyle, there's a test for his age group called—" there was a pause and Aaliyah heard more key clicking "—it's called an intellectual assessment scale. Oh, and here's another one. The Wechsler test. Both look to be specifically for his age group."

"Thanks, Lauren. Later tonight, I'll check those out."

That was the plan. But the night got busy and so did the days ahead. The video continued to draw attention. When a flurry of comments suggested the video had been staged and Kyle had been given the answers to memorize, Aaliyah was contacted by a local TV reporter and asked if his team could provide their own set of problems for Kyle to solve and film the results. She agreed.

Two days later, Aaliyah managed to get two hours of her shift covered so that she could take Kyle to the television station. There, Kyle was treated like a mini-celebrity as they prepared a series of complicated addition and subtraction problems on a whiteboard. The producers confirmed, on camera, that no one outside of those filming the project had seen the numbers. As he'd done on the previous video, Kyle studied each set of numbers for a few seconds and then simply wrote down the answer. From left to right. Without any visible calculation, no finger counting, no carrying numbers over, nothing. It was the first time Aliyah had witnessed it. The moment brought tears to her eyes.

"That's amazing, Kyle," the popular reporter said, after he'd fact-checked the answers using the calculator app on his cell phone. "How do you do it?"

Overwhelmed by the lights, cameras and extra attention, Kyle shrugged. "I don't know."

"If adding by longhand, most of us do it this way." The reporter walked over to the board, wrote 250 + 250 on it and then tabulated the way the average person did, by carrying the one from the second column's five plus five to show that two plus two plus one equals five, for the sum of 500. "But you don't do it that way, Kyle. You write the answer from left to write. How do you figure it out so fast?"

"I…" He fidgeted, looked at Aliyah.

"Don't be nervous, son. Just explain as best you can."

"I just see the numbers and I know the combinations, the answers. So I just add the first number to the number on this side—" he pointed to the left "—and then I write it down."

The reporter looked into the eye of the camera. "Did you get that, folks? Yeah, right. I didn't, either. And that's what makes this kid so special. We're going to keep our eye on you, Kyle. You're going places. And if you're going places, you'll want to stay tuned for the traffic report, after this."

After taking pictures with Kyle and the production team, the reporter approached Aliyah. "I must tell you, ma'am. I didn't believe that video for one minute. But your son proved me wrong. I really meant what I said to the viewers. You have a very special kid there."

"Thank you. I think so, too."

He pulled a card from his side pocket and handed it to her. "If I can be of any assistance in helping his star rise… I will definitely do my part."

The segment aired locally, on the MBC evening news. The next day, it was repeated on the network's national morning news show, *This Morning*. After that, it seemed that everyone Aliyah encountered, from the campus to the medical center to the grocery store, knew about Kyle. His peers at the community center thought he was a celebrity since he'd been on TV. Aliyah worried that all the attention might be too much for him to deal with. Goodness knew that with her already busy schedule, the increased phone calls she'd received had been a bit daunting. But so far, Kyle pretty much remained the kid he'd always been. Aside from the increased exposure, the TV interview had reminded Aliyah to look into intelligence testing for Kyle. He was in kindergarten now but who knew? Perhaps her son belonged in first grade. It was time to speak with a counselor who could help her chart his educational path and lay a foundation that guaranteed success.

On Saturday morning, mother and son did the usual—headed out for pancakes, Kyle's favorite. They entered the restaurant and were assailed.

"There he is!" The young woman who had frequently waited on them was beaming. "I saw your video, Kyle. Didn't know you were so smart!"

"What do you say, Kyle?"

"Thank you."

The other server joined them. "Well, look at this. We have someone famous joining us today!"

Various employees came over to speak with Kyle, even the cook and several customers came over. When their orders were taken, the server informed them it was on the house.

"Remember this lesson," Aliyah told Kyle when everyone left their table. "Being smart can take you far in life, and sometimes get you free pancakes!"

They continued to chat during breakfast. Aliyah was continually amazed at Kyle's view on various situations and circumstances he observed. He was able to articulate his position and even debate certain points. Her little boy was becoming a little man. She really enjoyed their conversation.

"Are you ready, Kyle?"

"Yes."

"What should we do next? A movie, or maybe a bookstore at the mall?"

"The bookstore!"

"Okay." Her phone rang. "Let me get this first. Hello?"

A brief pause and then... "Hello, Aliyah."

Hearing his voice made her stomach drop.

"Aliyah? Can you hear me? This is Ernest."

She took a quick sip of water, and prayed the egg white frittata she'd eaten didn't make a reappearance. "Hello."

"I'm sure you're surprised to hear from me. It has been some time since we've spoken."

"Yes." A simple answer, but while absorbing a spontaneous combustion of shock, awe and anger, it was the best she could do.

"How are you?"

"I'm fine."

"And school?"

"Good."

"Excellent. What do you have, two or three years left before you're Dr. Robinson?"

Seriously? The father of my child, whom I've not spoken to in almost three years is going to call out of the blue and expect me to happily join him in a casual chitchat?

"Why are you calling?"

"Mommy, let's go."

"One moment, son, okay?" She returned her attention to the phone call. "I'm in the middle of a few things. Is there a quick question or reason for your call?"

"Was that Kyle I heard? Is he there?"

Where else would he be? The moon? "Of course."

"He is the reason I'm calling, Aliyah. While I've supported him financially, I've come to the realization that money alone is not enough. He needs me. It is time for me to correct an error and reconnect with my son."

Chapter 16

"The mall is the other way, Mommy."

"I know, Kyle. Mommy has to go home and take care of something. I'm going to pick up Conner so the two of you can play together. Okay?"

"Okay."

Aliyah breathed a sigh of relief that the news about Conner satisfied Kyle's curiosity and shut down any more questions. She was still reeling from Ernest's unexpected phone call. The effort it had taken to remain calm had brought on a headache. She wouldn't be surprised if her blood pressure was sky-high. Feeling herself about to explode was why she'd ended the call and called Lauren, and was now making a beeline to her house. Five years later, and he wants to be a daddy? He'd had a realization? He qualified the monthly checks he'd send as support? Compared to the worth of both him and his family, what he'd sent Kyle over the years was a crime.

She needed to call back Ernest and get answers. Find out why all of a sudden he'd discovered a parental gene. But the conversation had to be private, without Kyle. And it would have to happen after she calmed down.

After getting the boys settled in front of a video game with snacks at the ready, Aliyah went into her bedroom and closed the door. "Breathe, Aliyah." She sat on the bench at the end of her bed, closed her eyes and worked to slow her heartbeat. Had she been able to sit still long enough, that might have happened. But she couldn't. Too much anger-fueled energy and boiling blood. She paced the length of the room, cursing out Ernest in her head, appalled at his nerve. She jumped when her phone rang, not yet ready to speak with Ernest, but determined to try anyway. She needed answers.

Good thing for her it wasn't him.

"Terrell. It's you."

"Who were you expecting? You almost sound relieved."

"I am. I thought it was Ernest, calling me back."

"Kyle's father?"

"Yes. After almost five years, he called and started chatting as though it was a perfectly normal thing to do." The memory alone made her livid. The pacing began again. "And then almost as casually informs me that through some recent revelation he now has clarity that his son needs him, go figure, and that it's time they connect."

"What did you say?"

"Fortunately, not what I was thinking. Kyle and I were having breakfast. I told him I'd call him. But I need a minute to get over the shock of hearing from him, and the anger at the presumptive, entitled attitude I heard when he talked about Kyle." She stopped pacing and took a breath. "Why is he calling? That, I did have time to ask. His answer? For my son! Really. What could have possibly happened to bring this on? Did he fall down, hit his head and suddenly remember he was a parent?"

"No. He probably saw him on TV, on the national morning show."

His answer hit her like a cold glass of water in the face. Of course.

"His calling caught me so off guard, I totally spaced. That's absolutely why he thought of us—the intelligent, charismatic, well-mannered son he's never met being on national TV. Now the timing of his calling makes sense. He didn't hit his head. He watched the morning news. So was the call about Kyle, or about the positive notoriety that is swirling around him right now? Is it because his son is being called a genius that he suddenly wants to claim parentage?"

"There's only one way to find out, Aliyah. You need to call him back, not to argue but to have a conversation and get an answer to all of these questions. You need to know what's on his mind."

The thought that some selfish motive and not love was what might have driven her ex to reconnect was too gut-wrenching to contemplate. It zapped her energy. She plopped down on the bed.

"I don't know if I can even deal with this right now."

"Do you think putting it off will make it any easier?"

"Not really."

"Then maybe you shouldn't. Who knows, it may not go as badly as you imagine." Aaliyah didn't know, and didn't answer. "Would you like me to come over for support?"

"No. But you're right. The sooner I have the conversation, the more information I'll have to make decisions. Your calling me was perfect timing. It helped to talk it out. Thank you."

"No worries. I've got your back. Call and let me know happened."

"I will." She ended the call, went out for a glass of water and to check on the boys. When she returned to the room there was no hesitation. She opened the incoming-call screen and tapped the number.

"This is Ernest."

"Ernest, it's Aliyah."

"Hello, Aliyah. I'm sorry to have caught you at a bad time earlier. Is everything all right?"

"Hmm...not exactly, to be honest."

"What's wrong?"

"You have no idea?"

"I'd rather not speculate, Aliyah, when you can just tell me."

"Okay." *Breathe, Aliyah. Discuss, don't argue.* "Your calling out of the blue is shocking to say the least, and your reason even more so. You say it is to reconnect with Kyle. For that to happen, you would have had to be connected with him in the first place. That is not the case. In fact, I can't think of anyone who tried harder to be disconnected from a child. First, through denial and then, through dismissal."

"Aliyah, it sounds as though you are still smarting over our breakup, perhaps even still wishing for something that can never be."

It was her first real laugh of the morning. After catching her breath, she adopted his proper tone. "Please rid yourself of such fantastical notions. The woman who believed herself in love with you has grown up and moved on. Kyle is who you denied, and after paternity was proven, still chose to dismiss from your life."

"It was not my choice, Aliyah. There were many factors involved in the decision. It wasn't a black-and-white issue."

"You're right. It was simply a black issue. A little black boy named Kyle issue, more specifically. That was the only factor to have been considered because it was the only one that mattered. Oh, wait, it was the only one that mattered to me. For you, money was clearly an equal consideration. That, and control. How do I know? Because what you spent on that cutthroat attorney could probably have paid for Kyle's college education. So please understand these issues, not wishful thinking, are why I may come off sounding a little perturbed."

"There's no doubt I've made mistakes in the past, but why are we rehashing that? I'm here now, and would like to move forward. I understand you've relocated to the west coast. That makes regular visitation more challenging—"

"Visitation? Did you mean to say introduction, because that's the first thing that usually happens with someone you've never met."

"You are right, Aliyah. And your anger is justified. I, too, have grown older and wiser, and in the process now acknowledge that regarding several matters better decisions could have been made. We can't go back into the past, so I've contacted you to fix the present. I want to get to know my son, Kyle. And as much as you may hate me, Kyle has a right to know his father."

She took a deep breath, and clenched her hands into fists to stop them from shaking. Belatedly, she realized that while water was good, a glass of wine may have been better.

"I'd like to ask you a question."

"Sure."

"After all these years, what made you call now?"

"It wasn't one single thing, Aliyah, but several."

"Such as?"

"Getting older, maturing, getting married."

"Right. You brought home someone your family found worthy."

"She is someone I've known since childhood. Our families have been friends for years."

At one time, the news of Ernest marrying would have been devastating. That now all she felt was sorry for his wife was proof that any romantic notion toward him was long gone.

"Have you by chance seen a recent video of Kyle?"

A hesitation, but only briefly. "As a matter of fact, I have! You remember Roosevelt, right? I believe he was about to get his doctorate when the two of you met. His wife is a PhD also, specializing in early childhood education. Someone brought the video of a so-called whiz kid to her attention, and she told Roosevelt about it. When he went online to view it, he clicked on another link that had aired on television, recognized you and contacted me. Given that I'd already planned to contact you, I felt the timing was a sign that my decision was the right one."

"Oh, so the television segment isn't why you called me. This was something you'd already planned."

"The facts are as I've stated, but nonetheless, my son's intellect is indeed impressive. Of course, given both yours and my level of intelligence, his high IQ is not surprising. My grandfather graduated high school at the age of fifteen."

Good for him. "Here's the situation, Ernest. While I agree that Kyle should know his father, the fact of the matter is he does not. I have told him about you, and showed him pictures. I am in agreement that you two should meet. But it needs to be at a pace that is comfortable for Kyle."

"Kids adapt quickly. He'll be fine. I would like to see him as soon as possible. Too much time has passed already."

The more things change, the more they stay the same. "Here's what I'm willing to do. I will consult with a child therapist trained in this area to learn the best way for us to proceed, and share those findings. I also need to know that this isn't a request predicated on a temporary desire. If you are not planning to be a part of his life for the rest of his life, then we can't go down this road."

"That choice and this journey is not up to you. Kyle is my son, legally and biologically. I will be a part of his life, and he will get to know the paternal side of his family. This can only happen through regularly scheduled visits to Rhode Island."

"That possibility is a long way from happening. Let's

start with the therapist and then something easy, like a telephone conversation. How's that sound?"

"Like a suggestion from one who's forgotten who I am, a man of means and ability to make things happen. I'm hoping we can resolve this amicably, but if necessary, legal action will be taken."

"I have full custody of Kyle, Ernest, and that is not going to change."

"We'll see about that."

"Yes, we will."

After a near-sleepless night filled with tossing and turning, Aliyah's anger had not waned. The nerve of Ernest! Calling her as if that were perfectly normal, something that happened all the time. Asking about a son that he at first denied and later abandoned. She hadn't seen him in three years, but was sure the size of his jeans had changed. It would take tailor-made ones to fit the ginormous *cojones* it took for him to call her. And his request? Regular visits? Across the country? Was he serious?

Unfortunately, Aliyah believed that he was. But when it came to her son and what was in his best interest, she would not back down.

Chapter 17

For once, Aliyah was thankful for the heavy three-day work schedule at UC Davis. She'd managed to transform anger into energy and give her patients the best care possible. Focusing on the management of their pain caused her to manage her own, and after a couple days had passed she was able to put the conversation with Ernest in better perspective. She'd also talked with a colleague who recommended a child therapist and had made an appointment. Taking this step made her feel better, too.

What didn't feel so good was not seeing Terrell. Dealing with Ernest had thrown off her entire weekend schedule. She'd canceled their Saturday night date to take Kyle and Conner to the movies. Sunday was filled with study and Terrell had had an event on Monday night. Several texts had been exchanged, but they'd talked only once in the past three days, and it was now late afternoon on Thursday. She missed him, but right now would forego Novocain and have a root canal before admitting it. Ernest's sudden reappearance in her life had brought up old memories, reopened old wounds and reminded her why she'd decided not to enter into a serious relationship right now. The most she would acknowledge was if she were to change her mind and want a commitment, it would be with a man like Terrell.

As if thinking him up, her cell phone rang. "Yes, I got your messages and was going to call."

"Good evening to you, too, Ms. Robinson."

"Hi."

"Busy?"

"Not at this very moment—am in between surgeries and was just checking my phone."

"I miss you."

She wouldn't say it back. She'd bite a hole in the side of her mouth first.

"No comment? Something like, 'I miss you, too,' or 'looking forward to seeing you'…something like that?"

"Nope."

"Dang, girl!" Terrell laughed. "Why you want to hurt me?"

"Your ego can take it. You're a big boy."

He paused, then said, "You still haven't told me about this past weekend, and how the conversation went."

"I know. It's been busy and I needed some time to think. But I will."

"I don't like how you sound, Aliyah. It's not just being tired. There's something else there. What is it?"

"I'll tell you later."

"Promise me you'll call tonight?"

"I promise."

Later, as soon as she'd put Kyle to bed and gotten comfy in her own, she did just that. "Hey, you."

"Um, the way you said that sounded so sexy, better than when we spoke earlier. How are you?"

"Better now."

"Of course. Because you miss me and now I'm here. You don't have to say it. I already know. Don't worry. The next time we're together I'll make up for this time we've spent apart."

"Gosh, you're smooth."

"And I mean every word. That's what counts. Now tell me about this knucklehead and what he wanted."

She did, the short version. "He didn't mention the video initially," she said, finishing up. "Only that he'd grown to realize the error of his ways and wanted to correct them."

"Do you believe that?"

"Not for a second. So I asked him straight out if he'd seen it."

"Has he?"

"Of course. And the fact that he didn't mention he'd seen it, that I had to bring it up, convinced me beyond all doubt that it's exactly why he called. In the past couple weeks, total strangers have come up to Kyle and me to talk about it. The waiters at the restaurant, even the cook came out to congratulate him. Our breakfast was on the house. People who've seen the video talk about it. So had the video been truly irrelevant, then saying he'd seen it would have been the first thing out of his mouth."

"Do you think he's serious about trying to get regularly scheduled visits established?"

There was silence as Aliyah pondered the question. "I think that this isn't solely his idea—that his wife and definitely his image/status/perception-conscious mother have been in his ear. When Kyle was simply the illegitimate child of a commoner, he had no value to the Westcott brand. But a child genius? Suddenly they can see themselves in him. He's become 'our child,' when before I was on my own. Now, he has the nerve to mention his grandfather, who graduated high school early, implying Kyle's intelligence is from their gene pool. His family is probably rethinking their stiff and vocal opposition to Kyle taking the Westcott name.

"If I know his mom, she wants to flaunt Kyle to her friends in a continued effort to prove their superiority. Not on my watch."

"Have you contacted your attorney?"

"Not yet."

"From what you've told me about this family, I suggest you do that ASAP. And I hope your attorney is ready for hardball because that is the type of game that's going to be played."

Terrell's words caused her another sleepless night. The Westcotts were used to winning and given his track record, the attorney she'd used before would be no match for their legal team. She'd need time and money to secure a comparable lawyer and she was short on both. There was never a good time for a custody battle, but now, in the middle of a fast-tracked residency program, was especially inconvenient. And ironic, given she'd always wanted Kyle to have a relationship with his father. But did Ernest really want to get to know his son, or was he capitalizing on being the father of viral video whiz kid? Time would tell.

She looked at the clock. Two hours until her shift at Living Medical. She went online to check her emails and search the web. But the thoughts persisted, too many to allow her to focus. Her nerves were too raw to sit still. So with Kyle having already been picked up by Lauren, she grabbed her purse and keys and headed out. Just as she reached her car and got in, her cell phone rang. It was one of her colleagues at the center. Due to a schedule mix-up, they were overstaffed. Lucky Aliyah had the day off.

More time to think. *Just what I needed.*

She called Terrell. "What are you doing?"

"Working. What about you?"

"I just found out I have the day off. This happens so rarely, I don't even know what to do with myself."

"I can think of more than a few things I could do with and to you."

"Ooh, sounds delicious. Want to play hooky?"

"I'll call you back in ten minutes."

He did it in five, and a short time later he picked her up and they went zooming down the freeway in his over-priced sports car. Top down, sun shining, hair blowing in the wind and singing hit pop songs loud and off-key. A spontaneous trip to Napa Valley was the perfect diversion.

"What's in Napa besides wine?"

"I don't know. Eating and drinking has been the extent of my experience."

She pulled out her phone and searched the web. "'Twenty things to do in Napa,'" she read. "Wineries, vine-yards, wineries in castles, vineyards on the hillside...ooh. We can take a balloon ride. Have you ever done that?"

"Can't say that I have."

"Can you say that you want to?"

"It might be fun."

"We could do a bike tour. Visit a museum." A phone call interrupted her search. Another unknown number, one of several she'd received since Kyle's video went viral. "Hello? Excuse me, who is this?" Terrell closed the convertible top. "Yes, this is Aliyah." She made a face, her eyes widening as she looked at Terrell.

What? he mouthed.

"That sounds excellent. I'm sorry, just a bit shocked right now." She listened, swatting at Terrell as he tried to get her attention. "Is that the only day available? Hmm. Then is there a way I can make a call or two and get back with you?" She mouthed something to Terrell. He couldn't seem to decipher the words. "I understand. I will call you back as soon as possible. Thank you! 'Bye."

As soon as she tapped the end button Terrell pounced, his expression a mixture of worry and curiosity. "What is it?"

"You are not going to believe this."

"What?"

"That was a producer from the Helen show."

"Helen DeMarco?"

"Yes! They've seen Kyle's video and want him to appear as a guest!"

"You're kidding?"

"This is crazy!"

Aliyah rarely had time to watch TV but knew that Helen was known for featuring talented kids on her show. Even she'd seen the adorable boy arguing with his mom about fixing her breakfast. He'd been invited to the show and given $10,000. He and several other of these guests had been found online.

"What's she say?"

"She said that someone had seen Kyle's video, showed it to Helen, and that was it. She told them to book him right away. There's only one problem." Her enthusiasm waned. "The show tapes in LA and they want us there Monday. I don't know if I can get the whole day off. But with all the logistics involved, I'd need it."

"If you tell them what's going on, I think they'll work with you. This is a big deal."

"I could ask Lauren."

"And miss being there for your son's debut on national TV. No, that's not going to work."

"You're right. It's not. Shoot! His assessment test is scheduled for Monday. And I'd planned to spend my day off researching lawyers. Who was the guy with the bright idea to videotape my son?"

"I tell you what, he's one smart brother. You owe him big-time. And he's definitely going to collect. Don't worry about LA, either. I'll help you get there."

"The producer said the network would buy my ticket. It's the added time of driving to and from either Oakland or San Francisco that makes this an all-day affair."

"We're not driving to either of those places."

"We're not?"

"That same smart brother I told you about has access to a private plane. He'll hook you up."

"Are you serious? And you'll come with us?"

"Of course."

She hit the call-back button. "Let me confirm with the producer and then call Mama. She's going to be so excited. This is her favorite show!"

Instead of choosing between the hot air balloon and bike tour, they did both. And Aliyah didn't think about Ernest or his visitation nonsense. Not even once.

Chapter 18

On Monday morning, Aliyah met Terrell at the regional airport.

"Good morning."

"Good morning, Ms. Robinson."

"Mr. Drake! What are you doing here?"

She got out of the car and opened the back door. "Come on, boys."

Kyle and Conner, who'd been invited along at Kyle's request, scrambled out of the backseat.

"What are you doing here, Mr. Drake?" Kyle repeated. "Are you coming with us?"

"Yes, Kyle, I am."

"Why?"

"We're flying to Los Angeles in Mr. Drake's plane, so we can get there faster."

Conner's eyes widened. "You have a plane?"

"The company I work for owns it. But I get to use it."

"Cool!"

"Where is it?" Kyle asked.

"Behind that building, on the runway. If everyone's ready, we'll go there now."

Once they were in the air and settled, with the boys being entertained by a friend of Stan's who was clocking hours toward his pilot's license, Terrell leaned over and snuck a kiss.

Aliyah gave him the side eye. "Don't. Start."

"I couldn't resist," Terrell replied, his sexy eyes still fixed on her mouth. "You look gorgeous. I like your hair loose and curly like that. You should wear it that way often."

"Thank you. It'll work for television but as a doctor, not so much. For that job, the good old ponytail is most efficient."

He reached over, grasped a tendril of her hair and rubbed it between his fingers. "Nice and soft. What I wouldn't do to…"

Pulling away, she gave him a warning between gritted teeth. "Behave!"

The petulant look he offered made her laugh out loud. "You are so silly."

"That's what you love about me."

An hour later, four excited Northern Californians landed at LAX. For the boys, the trip had been a great adventure, made extra special because of Stan, the pilot, who let each one come into the cockpit and "fly" the plane. Having Conner along proved to be a great distraction that prevented inquisitive Kyle from asking more questions about Terrell being there. There were more questions. Of this she was sure. His quick glances back to the two of them left no doubt.

The studio had arranged a car to meet them at the airport. Kyle and Conner kept up a steady chatter during the forty-five-minute ride from the Los Angeles airport to Hollywood and the studios where the Helen show was taped. They were ushered inside and led down a hallway to the greenroom, where one of the show's assistant producers joined them.

"Good morning, everyone!" Greetings abounded. "Flight okay, no problems?"

"No, it was fun!" Kyle said. "We got to fly the plane!"

A confused expression flitted across the producer's

face, but she just smiled and said, "Awesome!" She turned and kneeled. "You must be the famous Kyle Robinson!" He nodded.

"Speak up, Kyle," Aliyah said.

"Yes." His voice was just above a whisper.

"Kyle, don't be shy. Remember what Mommy said earlier? We have to speak…"

"Loud and proud."

"That's better."

"Good morning, Mommy," the producer said with hand outstretched. "My name is Jade, I'm here to take care of you, and walk you through the entire process so that everyone knows what's going on and can relax and have fun. Does that sound good?"

Everyone replied in the affirmative.

Turning to Terrell, she reached out to shake his hand. "Are you Kyle's father?"

This got Kyle's attention. Aliyah swallowed a moan.

"No. I'm Terrell Drake, assistant director for the Drake Community Center, which Kyle attends."

"And where this gift was discovered," Aliyah added.

"Well, we can't wait to hear all about that, but we'll save the details for in front of the camera. Right now, what I'd like to do is get both of you—" she looked at Aliyah and Kyle "—down to makeup and wardrobe—"

"Eww. I'm not wearing makeup!" Kyle's declaration was clearly not up for discussion.

"Are you sure?" Jade asked, clearly amused as Kyle vehemently shook his head. "You don't have to, young man. But the studio lights can get a bit warm. So they'll just take steps to make sure that you're not shiny and that your pretty mommy looks her best. That's a great color by the way," she said to Aliyah. "That your dress is maroon and not a loud red will read very well on camera.

Once they're finished in makeup, we'll come back here and wait for your cue."

"When will we meet Helen?" Aliyah asked.

"Not until you're introduced. She prefers to meet you just as the audience does, after you're introduced. That way the conversation is very organic and natural, as if she were meeting you for the first time…because she is! Any other questions?" She looked down. "Oh, I'm sorry, little one. I didn't introduce myself to you. What's your name?"

"Conner."

"He's my best friend!"

"Aww, that's nice. You came here to show support as Kyle makes his debut?"

"Yes."

"Well, that's a good friend. We'll make sure you have a front row seat in the audience. How about that?"

"It's good."

"Okay. As you can see, Terrell and Conner, there are snacks, drinks and, let's see, yes the *LA Times* is on the table. Feel free to help yourself to anything. Other than that, just relax and we'll be back in a half hour or less."

A short time later, Aliyah, Kyle and Jade stood just behind the curtain that opened to the soundstage for the Helen Show. Aliyah was struck by how ordinary and plain everything looked. To her, television was a world of glitz and glamour. She was expecting luxury, everything high-end. But backstage, at least, looked like any office, USA. She found it fascinating.

"You're on after this commercial break," Jade whispered.

Kyle looked at Aliyah. She reached for his hand and kneeled down. "You're going to do fine, baby. Just answer the questions like the little man you are. Okay?"

"Yes, Mommy."

As she listened to Helen make the introduction, a

woman she'd seen on TV and in magazines, the moment felt unreal.

"This kid," Helen continues, "makes me wish I'd studied harder in school and not played hooky during my math class. He does in his head what most of us can only do with a calculator. And I can't wait to find out how. Please join me in giving a warm welcome to the math magician… Kyle Robinson!"

They stepped from behind the curtain to thunderous applause. Aliyah was amazed at what she saw. All of the glitz missing backstage was on full display in every area caught by a camera lens. She felt Kyle's hand tighten on hers as they walked over to a smiling, standing Helen, who when they reached her, kneeled down and gave Kyle a hug.

"Have a seat, you two. It's great to have you on the show."

"It's great to be here," Aliyah replied. "What do you say, Kyle?"

"Thank you."

"So, Kyle. I've seen the videos of you working those long math problems in your head. People my age can't even do that, at least not without a calculator. How did you learn to do it?"

"I don't know."

"Did Mommy teach you, or is this something you learned in school?"

"Mommy buys me math videos for my tablet and I play with them. And then Conner's brother, Conrad, showed me, um, his homework for school. And it was math. And I asked him what he was doing. And he showed me. Then I said I wanted to do it. And he let me. And I got the right answer."

"Who's Conner?"

"My best friend. He's right there." Kyle pointed him out.

"Hi best friend, Conner," Helen said with a wave. "So Conner's brother is how old?"

"He's like…"

"Fifteen," Aliyah answered.

"Fifteen! You helped a fifteen-year-old do his homework?" Kyle nodded. "Boy! Where were you twenty years ago?"

The audience laughed.

"When did you get interested in numbers? Mom?"

Aliyah explained, starting with Kyle's early ability to count and his using building blocks to do simple math equations, to her downloading the first numbers-oriented games and increasing their difficulty as he continued to master them.

"But I had no idea he was at the level all of you are seeing," she explained. "I'm just as surprised as you are."

"How'd you find out?"

"Through the Drake Community Center in Paradise Cove. I'd enrolled Kyle there for tutoring, mentoring and other activities they offer. His teacher, Mr. Adams, saw a paper with math problems on it that had been left in his classroom somehow and noticed that the handwriting of the answers looked very elementary. He asked his five-and six-year-old students if someone had done it. And Kyle raised his hand.

"Mr. Adams didn't believe it, came up with some more problems, watched Kyle solve them and still couldn't believe it. That's when he contacted Terrell Drake, the assistant director, who was also floored. Terrell—Mr. Drake—contacted me asking how I'd taught him to work math that way. I had no idea what he was talking about so he shot a quick video to show me. That's how this all started."

"Such an incredible story, it really is," Helen said, as the audience applauded. "Kyle, are you ready to do some problems here, for the audience?" Kyle nodded. Helen stood. "Well, let's go over to the board, buddy, and do some math!"

The audience applauded, oohed and aahed as Kyle correctly answered the math problems Helen wrote on the whiteboard. Aliyah looked on as the proud mom that she was and gave Kyle a big hug when he rejoined her on the love seat.

"I tell you what, Kyle. You're going places! And I'm not the only one who thinks so. Some pretty important people and friends of the show have also seen your video. They've come here to meet you and to offer something I think is pretty cool. Everyone, please help me welcome a staff member from one of the top-ranked college math-and-science programs in the country. From the Massachusetts Institute of Technology, it's Mark Oberman!"

A handsome, bespectacled gentleman who appeared to be in his midforties came out to the sound of applause. He shook hands with Aliyah and Kyle, and gave Helen a hug before being seated.

"Mark, what do you think about Kyle, here? Pretty amazing stuff, huh?"

"Absolutely," Mark replied. "It is exciting to see someone so young so incredibly gifted." He turned to Kyle. "Good job, young man."

"Thank you," Kyle said, shaking the hand offered to him.

"Mark's not just here to congratulate you. He has something else he wants to say, but first—" she reached behind her and brought out a box "—we thought you might like a new video player to try out on your flight home."

Kyle jumped up, more animated than he'd been all morning. "Thank you!"

"It's loaded with all sorts of fun math stuff—equations, algebra, geometry...the stuff that gave me the heebie-jeebies when I was in school, but that you'll probably enjoy."

"Thanks!"

"Thank you," Aliyah said.

"Mark has something as well. Mark?"

"Yes, Helen. As many of you know, MIT has one of the best-ranked math-and-science curriculums available. Our campus is filled with bright, energetic minds who thrive in a culture that supports their dreams and aspirations, and their intellectual gifts. We seek out these types of students, not only those in high school and ready to graduate, but those who, like Kyle, show great potential at an even younger age. When those of us in the math department viewed Kyle's video, we knew he was the type of student who'd do very well in our environment. So I'm here on behalf of the university to offer to Kyle a full, four-year scholarship to our undergraduate program."

The crowd broke out in wild applause. Aliyah sat stunned. Kyle's eyes beamed. He enthusiastically shook Mark's hand. Aliyah, batting away tears, gave Mark a hug. Helen segued into a commercial break. Kyle's official TV debut was over.

Back on the plane, with the boys totally engaged in Kyle's new game, Aliyah and Terrell sat in the back, unnoticed, holding hands.

"Thank you for what you did this morning," Terrell said.

"What did I do?"

"You gave me and our center a major shout-out on national television. That's huge."

"I had to. You and your center are the reasons I even know about my son's talent, that Helen found out about it and now, why I don't have to worry about his college education. Geez! I'm still in shock over that. Totally unexpected."

"Tell me about it."

"Wait until this show airs tomorrow. Mama will be beside herself. My phone will be ringing off the hook."

"What happened today is a very big deal."

"Yes," she said, her voice becoming lower as she looked at him with sultry eyes. "And you are a large part of why today happened. I'm very thankful for your taking interest in my son and his abilities."

"Well, you know, I kind of have a thing for his mama."

"Yes, she knows that. She kind of has a thing for you, too."

He leaned over and whispered, "I can't wait until my thing gets to hang out with your thing, so we can do some things…know what I'm saying?"

"Then we should make arrangements for that to happen as soon as possible. I'd hate to keep a good thing waiting."

Chapter 19

Terrell had been up since five and at work since six. Part of the reason was that business was booming. The other part was because for Terrell, like most Drakes, work was his passion. Ike, Sr. both encouraged and expected hard work and stellar results. And he'd led by example. Not only that, but Terrell had also agreed to act as consultant on a totally separate project not connected with Drake Realty. He was now up to his eyeballs in work, suddenly juggling both divisions of a very busy department. Good thing he was the man for the job.

"Excuse me, Terrell?"

He looked at the intercom, surprised to hear his assistant's voice this early. Then he looked at the clock and was shocked that it was already nine o'clock. He'd been crunching numbers and reviewing his former colleague's open prospect for three straight hours? No wonder his neck was stiff.

Reaching up to massage a kink, he responded. "Yes?"

"I have a Lauren Hensley on line one."

Lauren? Even with dozens of clients and hundreds of acquaintants, he could almost always put a face to a name. Right now, however, he was drawing a blank.

"Find out what company she's with, please."

"Sure, one moment."

He rolled his head from one side to the next, then stood and stretched.

"Terrell, she said she's Conner's mother, Kyle's best friend?"

"Oh, okay. Put her through." He sat, a frown creasing his brow. Why would she be calling him? Had something happened to Kyle? Or worse, Aliyah? He pushed the speaker button. "Terrell Drake."

"Good morning, Terrell. I hope I'm not bothering you too much to call you at work. I tried the center first and they gave me this number."

"No problem, Lauren. How can I help you?"

"It's about Kyle and Aliyah. You know his appearance on the Helen Show is airing soon."

"Yes, I'm aware of that."

"Well… I'm not sure if a lot of other people know about it, such as the friends he has at the center. So I thought it would be nice to put together a little celebration for Kyle, a watch party, for him and some of his friends. Aliyah is always so focused on work, so I thought a fun afternoon would be good for her, too. I'm calling you for two reasons. One, to invite you to join us. I know you and Aliyah are friends and that she'd love you to be there. And two, I'd like to invite some of his friends who attend the center and wondered how I can get an invite to them."

"First of all, Lauren, that's a great idea. Where do you plan to have this party?"

"I'm not sure. Probably Paradise Cove, because most of the kids who attend the center live in or near there. Maybe a pizza parlor or… I don't know. I need to go online and see what's available."

"Would you like to have it at the center? We've got the room and equipment to watch the video, and we'd also be willing to buy the refreshments and whatever else you need."

"Terrell, that would be perfect! Thanks so much!"

He reached for his cell phone and tapped the calendar app. "It's no problem. What date are we looking at?"

"We're talking real casual here so I thought as soon as this Saturday?"

"Okay. Tell you what. I'm going to call the person who's in charge of that age group and give him your number. His name is Luther Adams. He can help you get all of this set up and give me the details. Okay?"

"Yes, that's great. Thanks, Terrell. I'm sure Aliyah and Kyle will appreciate it."

"No problem." He disconnected the call and tapped Luther's name on his cell phone. "Hey, Luther, what's up, man?"

"Just another day at the office, bro."

"I hear that, man, and will make this quick. I'm calling to give you the number to a parent of one of your students. Her name is Lauren Hensley. Her son's name is Conner."

"Yeah, Kyle's friend."

"So you know who I'm talking about, obviously. She called because Kyle's appearance on the Helen Show airs today but she doesn't think a lot of his friends either know this or will remember to watch it."

"Kyle Robinson is going to be on Helen?"

"That's right, you don't know this. Everything happened so fast but yes, Aliyah got a call on Friday for them to fly up yesterday to tape the show. It airs today."

"He got invited because of the video?"

"Yes. Someone from her staff saw it, showed it to her and next thing you know Aliyah is getting a call."

"That's amazing."

"That's not all. Someone on the staff at MIT saw it and offered Kyle a full four-year scholarship."

"Get the heck out of here."

"I'm serious."

"How do you know all of this?"

Terrell grimaced at the question. Most of the time, he forgot that he and Aliyah seeing each other was on the down low. "Because of time restraints, I offered Aliyah use of the company plane, and then accompanied them as a Drake Center representative."

"A representative of the center, huh? Is that how you're defining your latest rap game? You forget I know you, right? When it comes to Aliyah, and that stacked body of hers, the center is not what's on your mind. Because if anyone should have been repping, it's me. I'm the one who manages that age group, and the one who told you about Kyle's math skills."

"That's true, and if another similar situation comes along, with more notice, I'll be sure to include you in the plan. But this was last-minute, late Friday afternoon. Because of her schedule, she didn't think she could make it. That's why the company plane was offered, and why I went along. That and the fact that this gives the center some excellent publicity."

"So you were with her late Friday? I see the rap skills are working. Man, Drake. I wish I could bottle and sell whatever potion it is you slip these women to make them fall for you."

"Just taking care of professional business, brother. Just doing my job. Speaking of, Conner's mother, Lauren, wants to put together a little watch party there at the center. Something casual, I'm thinking the rec room with the big-screen TV—with light refreshments, you know, pizza and drinks or something like that. She wants to do it this Saturday, so my first question is whether or not you're available this weekend, and secondly if you can be at the center because I'm not sure I can and someone from staff has to be on site."

"I don't think we have anything going on. I'll have to

check with the wife to be sure. I'm curious, though. Why did she call you?"

"Probably because she met me at the festival on Halloween and knows I'm the AD at the center. She wanted to be sure and invite his friends, who mostly go there. At any rate call her and handle it. Whatever you two decide is fine. Just tell Miss Marva I've approved the event and will have my assistant put in the proper paperwork later on."

"All right. I'll take care of it. But don't think I'm not aware of your change in attitude when it comes to the shorties. I thought you were allergic to kids."

"When I have to be around them, I take an antibiotic."

"Yeah, one called Aliyah."

"Ha! Don't hate the player, bro. Hate the game."

"When it comes to that sister, you might want to think about retiring from the game. That girl is beautiful. And studying to be a doctor? If you were smart, you'd get serious and start dating her. Real talk. You're not getting any younger. Keep on going down this playboy road and you'll end up being the old man in the club, wearing a polyester suit and a bad hairstyle, trying to talk to women who could be your daughter."

"You know what, Luther? For the very first time since I've known you, brother, you just might be right."

Chapter 20

Aliyah stood chatting with a few of the other mothers as workers at the center began the party cleanup. When she saw movement from the corner of her eye, she turned to see Luther approaching.

"Excuse me, ladies." She took a few short steps to meet him. "Luther, thanks again for your all you help in putting this together, and coming in on a Saturday to oversee it all. I really appreciate it."

"It was no problem, Aliyah. Glad I could help."

"I means a lot. I've never seen Kyle so happy, and I enjoyed myself as well. This is a wonderful program."

"I agree, and that's due in large part to Terrell and the vision the Drakes had when this center was built. They put a lot of their own money into making sure that the building and everything in it were first-rate. He was supposed to be here, matter of fact." Luther's expression was one she couldn't quite read, but one that suggested there was more to this simple statement than met the ear. "Wonder where he's at?"

She wondered, too, had been looking forward to seeing him. Probably more than she should have. This week, the tables had turned. It had been Terrell working long hours and cutting short their phone conversations. It was she who'd asked him for a late-night rendezvous and him passing with the excuse of too much work. Her disappointment and melancholy feelings at their not being together forced her to admit to herself what she'd probably deny to others. She was falling in love with Terrell, and had been since the first day they met. Not that she knew what could come of this emotion. When it came to her schedule, she was looking at another couple of years of crazy. Now, with Terrell's likely promotion, he'd be working around the clock. Would the blaze of desire burning inside them be able to withstand long absences and time apart? Would he lose interest in her, or worse, meet someone else? Not long ago, she'd dismissed the possibility of anything serious happening between them. Now, at least privately, she could admit that if he wanted to take this friendship to another level, she wouldn't refuse.

But of course, no one could know this, least of all Luther, who Aliyah knew was not just a coworker but a friend. To the outside world, Aliyah hoped her face conveyed a message that she couldn't care less.

With the room almost empty, Lauren walked over and joined them. "Excuse me, guys." Then to Aliyah she said, "I'm heading out, kiddo."

"Me, too. Luther, thanks again. Kyle will see you Monday." She turned to Lauren. "Where are the boys?"

"On the playground. They just ran out and I told them they could stay there until I came and got them."

"Okay, let's go."

They walked to the playground where a few children, including their two boys, played. "Wait." Lauren placed a hand on Aliyah's arm to stop her. "I wanted a minute before we got the boys to talk with you and make sure you're all right."

"I'm fine. Why wouldn't I be?"

"Aliyah." Lauren fixed her with a look. "I know you were expecting Terrell and looking forward to him being here. He said he was coming. I don't know what happened. Had Luther talked to him?"

"I didn't ask. It's okay, Lauren. Really."

"Hey. How long have I known you? Since you were what, fifteen or sixteen? I've been with you through every jerk who came your way. I know when you're feeling a guy, and you're in way deep with Terrell Drake. And personally, I think that's great. I like him, Aliyah. I think he's a catch. So a little advice that you didn't ask for? Don't be afraid to love him. Hey, why don't I take Kyle with me? You can call him and maybe get together?"

"Thanks, but no. This will give me time to spend with my son. He's the male who needs my attention."

Aliyah's phone rang. She checked it. Terrell. "Hello?"

Lauren walked over to get the boys.

"Hey there, sweetheart. I meant to call you earlier but I ended up in an impromptu meeting and didn't get the chance. Are you still at the center?"

"Yes, but we're getting ready to leave."

"Who's we?"

"Kyle and I, and Lauren and Conner are also here."

"Any chance she can watch Kyle so that you can come over to my place? I'm still at work, and will be here for another hour at least. But I'd sure love to know that when I get home, you'll be there waiting."

Lauren followed the boys out, a questioning look on her face. Kyle and Conner ran ahead.

"Can you hold on a minute?" Aliyah muted the call.

"Is that who I think it is?"

Aliyah thought to be deceptive, but knew there was no use. Lauren knew her as well as anyone. "Yes."

"So…want to rethink my offer and let Kyle come with us?" Her face was one big smirk.

"I hate you when you're right."

They both laughed. Lauren slowly walked away but said

over her shoulder, "If you want keep your happiness a secret, you might want to turn down that glow."

"Hey, Terrell. That was Lauren. She's taking the boys."

"Yes! I'm going to get some tonight!"

"You are silly."

"Girl, my balls are about to turn blue." She laughed.
"And I think I'm going blind in one eye."

Aliyah continued chuckling as she walked to her car.
His jokester side was cute, but that he'd obviously not been
with anyone else was what really had her giddy. "What
time should I meet you?"

"Let's have dinner first. I'll pick the place and text you."

"Sounds good."

Later that evening, Aliyah pulled into the Paradise Cove
Country Club parking lot and texted Terrell her arrival, as
he'd requested. Within minutes, he was opening her car
door and warming her with his embrace.

"Um, you smell good."

"Thanks." A car door slammed. She abruptly pulled
away and watched as shortly afterward a well-dressed couple walked by them. They greeted Terrell warmly. Behind
them was another woman—young, beautiful—whose look
was blatantly seductive as she also spoke. He responded,
but his focus was on Aliyah. "You okay?"

"I'm not very comfortable in the country club setting,
and definitely not up to watching women flirt with you
all night."

"Ashley flirts with everybody. But you don't have to
worry about any of that." He offered his arm. "Right this
way."

They bypassed the sidewalk to the main entrance and
went around the building to a side door, which Terrell unlocked with a key on his keychain. He motioned Aliyah inside and placed his hand at the small of her back as he led

her down a hallway to a set of double doors, and opened it. "After you."

She stepped inside and stopped short, shocked at what appeared as a wonderland before her. The room was small, intimate, with a table set for two. The ivory-colored walls and deep burgundy-and-gold decor enveloped her in luxury. Dozens of white candles shimmered beneath large crystal chandeliers. Breathtaking.

She turned, her look questioning. "What's all this?"

"To apologize for missing your party, made private because I also remember how you don't like uppity crowds."

He reached for her hand and led them over to the table. They sat. Aliyah continued to look around, conflicting emotions blocking her words. This man was everything she'd ever dreamed of and more, yet a part of her was still guarded against becoming too close. The part that bore the scars of past pain was waiting for the real rich, successful guy to show his true, arrogant, condescending colors. The ones that Ernest and all of his friends had eventually shown her.

"Terrell, this is so thoughtful. I don't know what to say."

The door opened. A waiter carrying a champagne bottle approached.

"You can take time to think about it after the toast."

"Good evening, Mr. Drake. And you, miss."

"Cliff, this is my lady friend, Aliyah."

"It is a pleasure, ma'am."

"I've known Cliff all my life."

Aliyah smiled. "The pleasure is mine."

Cliff popped the top, poured each a frothing flute of bubbly and quietly left the room.

"Do you know every single person who lives in this town?"

"No, but I probably know over half of them." He held up his glass. She did, too. "To you, Aliyah Robinson, for being an amazing woman, an up-and-coming doctor and an outstanding mother who's raised a genius for a son."

"Aww, that was sweet." She leaned over for a kiss. "Thank you."

As they toasted, Cliff returned with a tray of fresh-baked rolls, spiced butter and paper-thin strips of veal. Each helped themselves to the appetizer.

"This is so good," Aliyah said after her first taste.

"The chef was lured away from a top-rated restaurant on the east coast and has been here about ten years. Everything he cooks is first-rate."

"Just so it doesn't bug me all night, who is Ashley?"

"The girl we saw coming in?"

"Is there more than one?" She smiled to cover the jab. Or investigation, depending on how one viewed it.

"Not in this town, that I know of. Your question came out of nowhere so I was just making sure."

"If you don't want to answer—"

"No, not at all. You can ask me about anybody we meet because more than likely I'll be able to fill in the background. Ashley pretty much grew up here. I've known her since I was around twelve, or so. She dated Niko off and on for years, until he met Monique. Shortly after that she hooked up with a guy in Los Angeles. Until tonight, I thought that's where she was."

"So she liked your brother, not you?"

"She liked all of us and to answer the question that's really on your mind, yes, I've been with her before, along with half the guys who live here. I'm not ever going to lie to you, Aliyah. I'm a grown man and I've been doing grown-man things since I was thirteen. I've been with a lot of women, most of them casually. The one time I was in a serious relationship, I didn't sleep around. And even though you refuse to use the *R* word, I'm not sleeping around, looking around or interested in any other woman right now. You've got my attention, baby. That's all I'm saying."

Aliyah exhaled and took a sip of champagne. "I've got a confession to make."

"Okay."

"I can't believe I'm making it but…" Another drink of courage. "Even though it was meant to be casual, the feelings I'm beginning to have for you aren't casual at all. They're deep and hopeful and quite frankly scare me to death."

"Because…"

"Because I've only felt this way one other time, and it ended badly. People assume otherwise but when it comes to men and dating, I don't have a lot of experience. At first it was because of college, I needed a scholarship and put all of my attention toward getting good grades. Then one of my then best friends got pregnant at sixteen and it totally changed her life, but not in a good way. That experience was my birth control throughout the rest of high school because I had no interest in going down that road and tempting fate. Which is probably why I fell so hard for Ernest and placed such value in him and his opinion. I tried so hard to make everything perfect. That's the type of person I am, I guess. When I'm involved in something, it's all the way, a hundred percent, you know? And I'm trying to hold back on how I feel, because…"

"Because, why?"

"Because now is not the time for me to attempt a relationship and even if it was, you're not interested in having one."

"How are you so sure?"

"Because that's what we both said when we met."

He reached over, took her hand and rubbed a comforting thumb across her palm. "What if I told you I'd changed my mind? What if told you that I'm feeling you just as much as you're feeling me? Would you take a chance on this being a relationship?"

"Terrell, I don't know. There's already so much going on and I don't want this to be complicated."

"It doesn't have to be hard. It can be as easy as you finally admitting what I've known for a while."

"What do you mean, that you've known?"

"Girl, I know you're in love with me. I put that Drake on you, baby. You couldn't help it."

Aliyah huffed. "Wow, really? What an arrogant thing to say!"

Terrell smiled and kissed her hand. "I thought that's what you loved about me."

Chapter 21

Amazing what honesty could do. Terrell's pride soared at being one she could trust. She'd not only faced her fears, but also allowed herself to be vulnerable by voicing them. In that moment, the dynamics shifted. The walls came down. And feelings deepened. It took some convincing, but he talked her into returning to the Drake estate, and spending the night. Now however, in the clear light of morning, Aliyah's initial reservations of spending the night in his parents' home came back full-force. Terrell's inviting her to stay for Sunday brunch brought on a full debate.

"It's not like you haven't been here before."

"That was different!"

"How so?"

"Because first of all, I didn't know before I came over that it was your parents' house. And secondly, I left in the middle of the night. They never knew I was here."

"Are you sure?"

Aliyah looked grief-stricken. "You told them?"

Her reaction made Terrell laugh loud, and earned him a punch on the arm.

"That's not funny!" It actually was, kind of. As long as it was a joke. Otherwise, she would have been mortified. Her mother was no prude, but she would have been had Aliyah brought over someone to spend the night—it would not have been okay and it definitely would have not been in her room. Ernest's family, the Westcotts, were even worse. During their three-year courtship, she'd stayed twice at their family manse. His mother, Cordelia, put her in a guestroom so far from where Ernest slept that they might have been in different zip codes. Even so, she'd had the nerve to knock on her door at midnight under the pretense of having heard a noise. That lie was as see-through as freshly cleaned glass. No doubt she was sure Aliyah had snuck into her pious son's room with a potion to taint him and take his virginity. He was nowhere near virginal, but you couldn't tell Cordelia that about her son. In fact, she spoke so harshly against being intimate one would think Immaculate Conception was how Ernest arrived.

"You didn't tell them, right?"

"No, but had I done so it wouldn't have been a problem. Just like it's not going to be a problem today."

"I can't do it. I cannot waltz down those stairs after being intimate with their son under the same roof, and meet your parents for the first time! That's just too embarrassing."

"My parents won't judge you. They're not like that. Last night, you did acknowledge this was a relationship, right?"

"That is correct."

"Then it's time to meet my folks." Aliyah scrunched down and covered her head with the sheet. "Okay, I've got an idea. Instead of taking the stairs we can exit through the side door and enter through their front door. It will be as though you just arrived."

She slowly pulled the sheet away. "I appreciate the invitation, Terrell. Really, I do. Being with you and what I've experienced when meeting those in your family that I have so far is as different as night is from day to my time with the Westcotts. It's helped to further heal that part of me that was so destroyed by their callous behavior. It means a lot and I want you to know I'm grateful."

"Why do I feel a *but* coming? And not the one I always enjoy when it comes my way?" He reached for her backside.

She scooted away from him and sat up. "I want to meet your family. But not today. And not like this, sneaking around and being deceptive. Acting as though I've just arrived when I'm probably wearing a JHS face."

He frowned. "What's that?"

"A just-had-sex face."

"Girl!" He reached for her again. She dodged him, laughing, and jumped out of bed.

"Come back here!"

She tried to shut the bathroom door but he was quicker. "Out! I've got to use it."

"Not until you promise me something."

"I mean it, Terrell. Give me some privacy. I've got to use the bathroom!"

"Not without your word."

"Okay, what?" Aliyah squirmed as she tried without success to push him out the door. Like trying to move a stone statue bolted in concrete. "What?!"

"That you'll join us for Thanksgiving."

"Okay. Now get out."

"Both you and Kyle."

"Okay, fine." The squirming had turned to hopping. Not cute.

"No. Promise me."

"Terrell!"

"Do it."

"Okay, Silky, I promise. Thanksgiving. Now move before I pee on your floor!"

She tried to get out of it. In the week and a half since Aliyah promised to spend Thanksgiving with Terrell's family she'd come up with every reason possible to renege on her vow. He was having none of it. He'd even called her later that night and confirmed, made sure that she was not scheduled for work that day, both jobs, and school, so that later she couldn't use those excuses. Like now. When she seriously wanted to act like a woman and change her mind. Silly, she knew, to feel trepidation about spending the holiday with the Drakes. Especially after Terrell had explained that the day would be less formal than at other times and held outside, at Warren's ranch, and called for casual attire. They'd even invited another family with kids Kyle's age, just to make sure her son was comfortable. Terrell really had thought of everything. If she wasn't so sure about this not being the time for a relationship, and him not being the type of man to have a relationship with, she could see herself up and falling in love with him. Yep, hook, line and sinker. If she weren't so sure that she wouldn't.

With a last look in the mirror, and final self-approval that the flowing peach-colored maxi with fall-colored leaves paired with wedged brown ankle boots and a belt of the same leather was just the right amount of casual and chic, she stepped out of her bedroom and into the living room, where Kyle sat watching TV.

"Are you ready, Kyle?"

"Yes."

"You look quite handsome today." She turned off the television and lights, and set the alarm.

"Thank you."

"Grab your jacket. It might get cold later." She reached for a gift bag, and the shawl beside it. "We're going to meet Mr. Drake's family. I want you to be on your best behavior, okay?"

"I always behave, Mommy."

She smiled. "You're right, son. Mostly, you do."

A short time later she pulled into the wide expanse of concrete and gravel that served as Warren Drake's driveway. Several other cars, SUVs and a Jeep were already parked there. Music and the sound of voices floated from behind the house out to greet them, stirring up Aliyah's belly of butterflies. She pressed her hand against her stomach and with a last look in the rearview mirror exited the car, grabbed Kyle's hand and headed down the path toward the sounds.

As soon as they'd reached the end of the path and turned the corner, Aliyah saw a familiar face.

"Aliyah, hello! Welcome back."

"Hi, Charlie." The two women shared a warm embrace. "I hope we're not late."

"Not at all. They all came early," she said, tossing her head in the direction of four tables of six, and a bit farther away a kiddie table for four. "You know how family can be. No manners at all." She looked at Kyle. "Hello, little fella."

"I'm not—"

"Kyle." Her stern voice and slight hand squeeze squelched the oncoming argument. "Miss Charlie knows you're five. She meant that as someone not as tall as her."

"Absolutely," Charlie agreed, with a quick wink to Aliyah. "You're on a ranch, son. Around here you're not big until you're at least three hands. To a horse, know what I mean?"

He shook his head. "You have horses? Mommy, can I ride the horse?"

"What makes you think you can ride a horse?"

Both Aliyah and Kyle turned around.

"Mr. Drake!"

"Hey, buddy. Hello, Aliyah." He gave Kyle a high five and Aliyah a slight hug.

"Are you just getting here?" Aliyah asked.

"No. I went over to Teresa's real quick. She and Atka just arrived this morning. They'll be over in a bit. Come on, let's go meet everybody. Starting with Becky!" A young, petite woman with twins in tow stopped in front of them. "Becky, this is my friend Aliyah and her son, Kyle. Kyle, these are Becky's children, Matt and Melinda. They're five years old, too. And big, like you."

"Hi, Kyle." Becky turned to her children. "Say hi, guys." They did. "Kyle, would you like to come with us? We were just heading down to the barn to feed the pony."

"Ooh, can I, Mommy?"

"Of course. Don't run! Stay with Miss Becky!" She watched him run off, chattering away with Matt. "And here I thought it might take him a while to warm up to new kids."

"It did. About five seconds after the word *pony* was spoken." He reached for her hand. They walked over to a table of chatting adults, whose conversation stilled as they approached.

"Everyone, I'd like you to meet Aliyah Robinson. She's here along with her son, Kyle, who's already gone cowboy and went to ride a horse."

Aliyah turned to him with a worried look. "They're not going to actually ride it. Are they?"

"Don't listen to Terrell. He's always teasing." Aliyah smiled at the attractive woman with a flawless complexion, sparkling teeth and eyes, and a hand outstretched. "I'm Terrell's mother, Jennifer. Pleased to meet you."

"And you, Mrs. Drake."

"No need to be so formal, dear. Jennifer is fine. This is my husband, Ike, our dear friends and neighbors, Chet and Bonnie Donnelly, and Charlie's family who are also her and Warren's neighbors, Alice and Griff."

"It's nice meeting everyone, though I doubt I'll remember all of your names for more than five minutes. But please, don't hold it against me."

"Terrell tells me you're in your residency to become an anesthesiologist?"

"Yes, Mrs. Drake, um, Jennifer. I am."

"Then it's a wonder you remember your own name sometimes. We will forgive you."

Aliyah gave a quick nod, and a smile she hoped belied her nervousness.

It did not.

"No need to be nervous around us, Aliyah. We can be a rowdy bunch at times but it's all bark. No bite—" she lowered her voice conspiratorially "—unless we're backed into a corner and then we'll snap off your head!"

Aliyah exhaled on a wave of laughter. Less than a minute in and she knew Terrell was right. The Drakes were nothing like the Westcotts. By the time they'd made it around the yard, meeting the rest of Terrell's family and other guests, Atka and Teresa had arrived along with Aliyah's appetite, which had been overtaken by butterflies.

The catered affair was happening buffet-style. After fixing their plates, Aliyah and Terrell joined Charlie, Warren, Teresa and Atka at one of the tables. After a few general questions to and about Aliyah, Charlie turned their attention to Kyle.

"Have you guys seen her son on YouTube?"

"Yes, and it's phenomenal," Teresa replied.

"He's a mathematical genius," Charlie went on. "Was on the Helen show and got a scholarship to MIT!"

Jennifer, seated at the table next to them, overheard. "MIT?"

"Yes," Charlie answered.

"How'd that happen? Sorry, but I didn't start eavesdropping until midway through the story."

They laughed. Aliyah turned her chair slightly to make eye contact with Jennifer. By the time she was finishing up with the quick version of the story, everyone was listening.

"I wish I could take credit," Aliyah said. "I did notice Kyle's fascination with numbers and encouraged it with puzzles and later video games. But what you guys are see-ing on video and television was as much a surprise to me as it was to you."

Niko's wife, Monique, wiped her hands on one of the monogrammed linen napkins, which even though they were in a backyard, seemed quite appropriate. "But who taught him how to add and subtract such huge numbers? Surely that didn't come from the games alone."

"No, the video games and the creative math exercises were only the beginning. It was a teenager named Con-rad, the older brother of Kyle's best friend, who worked with him on solving larger problems. But even he had no idea Kyle had taken it as far as we all now see that he has."

"As far as an exceptional education," Jennifer ex-claimed. She held up her glass. "I believe that great op-portunity deserves a toast." Everyone raised their glasses. "To Kyle, a smart young man with a very bright future being raised by an obviously very smart mom."

"Hear! Hear!" The cheers rang out as glasses clinked.

"I appreciate that, Jennifer," Aliyah said, once the voices had quieted. "But I also have to give some of the credit to Terrell. After all, he's the one who videoed him and suggested I put it online. Had that not happened, we wouldn't be having this conversation."

"Interesting," Jennifer replied, eyeing her son over a glass of sparkling wine. "I've never known Terrell to take much of an interest in young children. That he's involved at all is quite noteworthy."

"Mom, if you're going to try and fish for information right in front of me, the least you could do is hide the pole."

"Son, I am merely stating an observation. And what-ever secrets you think you have… I already know them."

"Whoa!" Niko said. "Man, you know you can't pull any-thing over on Jennifer Drake." Then to Aliyah he asked, "Do you work at the center?"

"No, I'm in residency at UC Davis."

"Ah, a doctor?" Ike, Jr., who'd spent most of the conversation observing, chimed in for the first time.

"Yes, an anesthesiologist."

"Now that's a woman who can hang with Terrell," Ike, Jr. said. "If he gets out of line, she can just put his ass to sleep!"

The yard erupted with laughter and teasing. Terrell gave just as good as he got and Aliyah wasn't spared from the ribbing. By the time dinner was over she felt like part of the family. And to think her paranoia almost made her miss this good time and great family? Perish the thought!

After a day of food, fun and more laughter than her sides could handle, she pulled Terrell aside. "Babe, I should go. Kyle's getting sleepy and I owe my folks a phone call."

"You haven't called them today?"

"Yes, earlier, before I came here. But my mom called again this afternoon and I need to call her back."

They said their goodbyes. Jennifer insisted on walking with them to the driveway.

"Jennifer, your family is wonderful and the food was delicious. Thank you for making me feel so welcome in your home."

Jennifer gave her a light hug. "It was my pleasure, dear. You're welcome anytime, with or without my son." She watched as Terrell stopped to say something to his twin. "We've just met, but still, you are quite impressive."

"Thank you," Aliyah replied. "But anyone who studies diligently and works hard can become a doctor."

"Perhaps, but I'm not talking your being a doctor. I'm talking about your accompanying Terrell to a major holiday meal. Trust me, it doesn't happen often. And never has he chosen to invite a lady who's spent the night in our home."

Aliyah could have dropped dead right then.

Jennifer chuckled. "Oh, don't be embarrassed, dear. Very little happens in my coop and with my chickies that this mother hen doesn't know about. Just wait, you'll be the same with Kyle. I think spending quality time together is essential to getting to know each other. I look forward to knowing you more."

After making plans for the weekend with Terrell, Aliyah left with Kyle for the quick drive home, made even faster by his nonstop chatter. That he was impressed with ranch living was an understatement. Next year, he informed her, there would be no Avenger. Kyle was dressing up as a cowboy! Once home, the chatter stopped, and for her son sleep came quickly. With Aliyah, not so fast. But she didn't mind. She spent time on the phone with the family back east, enjoyed a quick chat with Lauren and even caught the last of *The Best Man*, her favorite movie. Through all of this, however, Aliyah's mind replayed the past several hours and the difference a day made. The switch had happened so quickly and subtly that she just now admitted it was true. When thinking of Terrell, she thought of the *R* word. And for the first time since she'd met him, she didn't run from the truth. She was in a relationship with a man she adored from a family that was simply amazing. Her heart was nearly bursting with joy and she couldn't stop smiling.

Until just before going to bed, when her cell phone rang and she checked her ID. Ernest. She let it go to voice mail.

Chapter 22

"Aliyah."

She turned around, looking up from the chart of her next patient. "Yes, Doctor?"

"Is it true that the whiz-kid video is your son?"

"You've seen it?"

"I think just about everyone in the hospital and on campus has seen it."

"Oh, my."

Aliyah was genuinely surprised. Juggling Ernest and Terrell, handling the eventual reentry of his father into Kyle's life and a booty call-turned-relationship on top of a work schedule on overload had taken all of her attention. But now, considering that the video had gone viral and her son had appeared on Helen, she shouldn't have been surprised.

She reached her next patient's room and stopped. So did the doctor. "My son is eleven years old and can't figure out those types of equations in his head. Everyone in his class uses calculators. Heck, I'm forty-five and can't figure them out that way. How does he do it?"

"I have no idea and quite frankly, neither does he. It's a gift."

Her phone vibrated. Unknown caller. An image of Ernest came to mind. She looked at her watch and let it go to voice mail. "Sorry, Doctor, but I've got to—"

"Me, too, but hey. Good work with Mr. Smith. He's an old codger and your bedside manner is exceptional."

"Thanks, Doc."

Three hours passed before Aliyah was able to take a break. Because she was gaining expertise in both pain management and cardiothoracic anesthesiology, cases often overlapped and left her little if any downtime between patients and procedures. Mostly she didn't mind it. Focusing on patients kept her mind off less pleasant thoughts. Like Ernest and what her mother had said when they'd talked last night. Her mother was right. Ernest had a right to know his son and vice versa. Aliyah agreed. His knowing Ernest wasn't the problem. It was the other West-cotts and their uppity thinking that she wanted to keep away from her impressionable son.

Still, right was right, so instead of going to the break room she headed to the exit and her car. On the way, she told herself that speaking with Ernest didn't have to be difficult. That if both were civil, polite and reasonable, appropriate arrangements could be worked out, including a cordial relationship to maintain for the sake of their child.

She reached her car, got inside and dialed his number.

"Thanks for finally deciding to return my call."

Not the best start, but she kept to her plan. "Hello, Ernest. I apologize for not calling earlier. It was a busy weekend, and I wasn't available."

"You work overnight now?"

Ignore, don't argue, she thought. "I'm sure you're calling about Kyle and visitation rights. While my reaction to your request hasn't been overly enthusiastic, I do want you and Kyle to know each other. It is in his best interest to know both sides of his family and I will do everything I can to insure his mental and emotional health."

"I'm glad we're finally on the same page. I can fly down this weekend."

"You coming here is probably best but this weekend is too soon. We still need to meet with the therapist."

"For what? What's wrong with him?"

"Nothing is wrong with anyone, Ernest. I just know that an experience like this can be very confusing, even upsetting for a child his age. I'm sure we both want to proceed in a way that is least likely to cause any unnecessary angst in his life."

"He's meeting his father, Aliyah, not a serial killer."

"He wouldn't know the difference." An immediate reaction that she'd have liked to have back. "I didn't mean that the way it sounded, Ernest. It's just—"

"Look, Aliyah. You've had five years to do with Kyle as you please. Those days are over. It is time for me to step in and place him on the path that as a Westcott, he must follow. And by the looks of things, I'm not taking action a moment too soon."

Civility flew out the window with politeness on its tail. "By the look of things? Are you serious right now? First of all, Kyle is a Robinson, not a Westcott, by your design."

"That will be rectified as well."

"Secondly, the only path Kyle must follow is where his heart takes him. His will not be a life dictated by an archaic and asinine set of societal rules. This is the page you and I will be on before Kyle is allowed out of my sight to be left alone with you or your family."

"And we should leave it up to you? Someone who thinks it's okay to parade a child on television like some trained animal?"

The comment knocked Aliyah back in her seat. "I must have heard incorrectly just now. You can't be talking about Kyle's appearance on Helen, the one that led to his having a full college scholarship."

"Yes, one that will disappear as soon as they figure out the trick you've used to make that possible."

"It's no trick, Ernest. Kyle is formulating those answers. Had you watched the show yourself instead of relying on secondhand information, as you've obviously done, you'd know this."

"No five-year-old can solve those types of math problems."

"At least one can."

"I don't believe you, and I will not have my son become a mockery. What happens with him is no longer up to you alone. I will have equal say in my Kyle's life."

"Eventually, perhaps. But right now, in this critical period of the two of you meeting, we're doing things my way."

"You think so?"

"I know so."

"We'll see."

"Ernest, I don't want to… Hello?" She looked at her phone. He'd hung up. The call had definitely not gone as she'd planned. Was she being unreasonable in wanting advice from a counselor? What if Ernest met Kyle this weekend and everything went fine? Question after question bubbled up in her head, driving her crazy. She placed another call.

"Good afternoon, Ms. Robinson."

"According to whom?"

"Hey, wait. I'm not looking at your booty!"

"Ha!" Terrell's remembering this as their very first exchange made her laugh out loud, something which under the circumstances was very hard to do. "Thanks. I needed that laugh."

"Why? Is something wrong?"

"Yes, but you're at work and undoubtedly busy. We can talk later."

"If there's a problem, we can talk now."

"Okay. I talked to Ernest."

"I take it the call didn't go very well."

"Not as I'd hoped. I wanted he and I to calmly, rationally discuss a plan of action for introducing him into Kyle's life, which, for me, begins with his seeing a therapist."

"Ernest?"

She laughed again. "No, silly. Kyle. Although on second thought the both of them being seen is not a bad idea. Maybe even the three of us in some type of family counseling. I just know that these types of situations can go really good or really bad depending on how they're handled. So rather than just jumping in with no forethought, I want us to have rules and a game plan, and having been the steady parent in his life until now, I believe I have the right to decide how this happens. Am I wrong?"

"I wouldn't say that you're wrong, however, I wouldn't be surprised if you aren't being overprotective, maybe more than is necessary. I also know that women sometimes use the kid to get back at the father. This isn't something I think you'd do consciously but…it happens."

"I want Kyle to know his father. With all the craziness associated with how he and I ended, the three years we were together weren't all bad."

"What was it about him that you found attractive? Because from everything you've told me so far, I don't see how he even got your number, let alone a date."

"This guy I'm dealing with now isn't the Ernest who approached me on campus. That guy was polite, intelligent and sure of himself in a way that a then nineteen-year-old girl hadn't seen before. He was my first real boyfriend—heck, my first real date. The boys in my neighborhood were focused on sex, hip-hop and easy money. Nice enough guys, but they could have cared less about calculus or the political climate or weightier topics that I thought about. Ernest and I could talk about anything and he wouldn't just listen. He'd actually have an opinion. I was so enamored that it took a while to realize that his became the only opinion that mattered even in relationship-oriented conversations where both viewpoints should have mattered. I didn't have anyone to measure him against and was too focused on school to give it much thought. Until that last year, when I met his parents. Their abject displeasure at his dating choice changed our dynamic immediately and completely. Once I got pregnant, and his inheritance was threatened, I saw a side of him that I didn't know existed. Or maybe it's just that I took off the rose-colored glasses."

"What are you going to do?"

"Apologize, for one thing. No progress can be made if this becomes war. I'll also schedule the therapy session as soon as possible. I'm really not trying to keep Ernest away from his son. The sooner the therapist gives the green light, the sooner their meeting can happen." She looked at her watch. "Thanks for listening. I feel better just having talked all of this out."

"I'm glad to hear it. I always want to make you feel good."

She smiled, opened her car door and headed back to the hospital. "Stop it with the sexy talk. You know what that does to me."

"Exactly why I'm doing it, babe. See you after work tonight?"

"You are so bad."

"I thought that's what you loved about me."

"I'll show you what I love about you, a little later on."

Chapter 23

Both Terrell and Aliyah had busy weeks so they had to settle for face time on Friday at the center. It would be brief. Terrell would only be there to sign a few documents and she'd be on her lunch hour, which by the time she arrived would be forty-five minutes because she was running late.

Her cell phone rang. Terrell, no doubt, who was as punctual as a Rolex. She pressed the car's answering device. "I know! I'm on my way."

"Where are we going?"

"Oh, uh, Ernest. Sorry about that. I'm on my way to a meeting and running late."

"Something for school?"

"No, it's a community center that Kyle attends."

"A community center?"

Determined this time to stay upbeat and on the high road, she ignored the slight sound of derision in his voice. "Yes. It's a wonderful, state-of-the-art facility in Paradise Cove, not far from Davis. They offer a variety of programs and activities along with tutoring, mentoring and just having fun. As an only child, it's been a great place for Kyle to learn interactive skills as well. He loves it there."

"What's the name of this place?"

"The Drake Community Center. Check out their website." Said because she knew that's exactly what he'd do.

"I think you'll be impressed. So, you got my messages—the apology, about Kyle's progress in kindergarten and the appointment for counseling being scheduled?"

"Yes, I did. But I'm afraid your schedule isn't going to work for me and my family."

Aliyah tensed immediately, her hands gripping the wheel. She took a deep breath and relaxed her fingers. Getting upset again was not an option. "I totally understand, Ernest, and when making the appointment asked for the very earliest date. She came highly recommended and is one of the top child therapists in the country, which I'm sure is why she's booked three to four weeks out."

"I'm not going to wait that long to meet Kyle, or introduce him to this side of his family. We're going to Martha's for Christmas and plan for him to join us."

She pulled into the center's parking lot and turned off the car. "I'm sure Kyle will love spending time at the Vineyard with your family, but there is no way that can happen in three weeks. Ernest, please know that I am not trying to be difficult nor keep you from your son. The two of you will spend lots of time together. But that's after he gets to know you, and feels comfortable enough for me to leave him alone in your care. Yes, you're his biological father. Yes, I am pleased that Kyle will get the chance to know his dad. But the truth of the matter is right now, in his eyes, you're a stranger. Can you understand that from his point of view?"

"Did you take him to see a counselor before leaving him at the center? Huh? Did you drag out the process and set up a bunch of roadblocks before those strangers took care of your kid?"

She exited the car and walked to the entrance. "My best friend's son, Conner, goes to this center. That's how I found out about it. Conner and Kyle are best friends and I knew that with someone familiar around him, he'd be fine. Even so, I did due diligence regarding their programs and faculty before he joined."

She reached Terrell's office, tapped his open door and entered.

"Good afternoon, Ms. Robinson. You're looking lovely today."

"Good afternoon!" She motioned for Terrell to hold a moment. "Ernest, I'm at my appointment. Can I call you later this evening?"

"You're at the Paradise Cove center?"

"The Drake Community Center in Paradise Cove, yes."

"Okay, then. No problem, sweets. We'll talk later."

She scrunched her brow as she ended the call. "That was odd."

"Talking to a knucklehead usually is. Have a seat." He reached behind him, took a carryout bag from the credenza and began removing its contents.

She sat. "Actually, believe it or not, that conversation with Ernest was relatively civil."

"Now, from what you've told me about him, that is odd."

She laughed. "I know, right. But more than getting along, he called me a pet name I haven't heard since before we broke up."

Terrell's hands stilled. "What did he call you?"

"Down, tiger," she joked, noting his change in demeanor. "Nothing bad. In college, I was known for always having some type of candy in my purse, book bag, pocket, wherever. He started calling me sweets."

"I knew it," Terrell said with a feigned sigh. "I'm going to have to beat a brother down for trying to step to my woman because she's the baby mama of his child."

"Ernest and I reconnecting romantically is the absolute last thing you'll ever have to worry about."

"For his sake, that's a good thing." He handed her a wrapped package. "Your gourmet lunch is served."

After wiping her hands with a sanitized cloth, she pulled the tape securing the paper. "Roasted turkey? With mayo and mustard?" Terrell nodded. "You remembered my pickles, too?"

"Just as you requested."

"Thank you."

"I bought us sodas from the cafeteria. Is cola okay?"

"Sure."

He handed her a covered, plastic cup filled with ice and soda. "Thanks, babe."

After a couple of bites, Terrell reached for a napkin. "I've been meaning to ask you something."

"What?"

"In our family, Christmas is a big deal. We don't choose names. Everybody gets something for everybody."

"That's nice."

"So what do you want?"

"Me? You don't' have to get me anything."

"I know I don't have to. But what do you want? Or let me word it a different way. When out shopping, what types of stores are you drawn to?"

"Usually the kind that allow me to go in, get what I want and get out in as little time as possible." She took a sip of cola. "I appreciate you asking but really, finding out what's really on Ernest's mind and then getting him to leave my life as quickly as he came will be gift enough."

They continued chatting casually, enjoying their lunch. She was just about to leave when a young man dressed in a navy blue suit knocked on Terrell's door.

"Yes?"

"Excuse me, sir. Are you Terrell Drake?"

"Yes. Come on in."

The man entered, his attention going from Terrell to Aliyah.

"How may I help you?" Terrell asked.

"Actually, I think she's who I'm looking for. Aliyah Robinson?" he asked with a smile.

Aliyah turned to him in surprise. "Yes, I'm Aliyah Robinson."

"Okay, great. Then this is for you." He handed her a white envelope.

Taking it, she asked him, "What is this?"

The smile left the stranger's face as he answered, "You've been served."

Before she could think to ask a question, he turned and left. She looked at Terrell, at the envelope, and back at him.

He held out a letter opener. "Only one way to find out what's inside."

"I can't imagine…" she began, before an image of Ernest's face came to mind. Her hands stilled, briefly, before she gave the opener a forceful pull and cleanly slit the top. Displaying a calmness she did not feel, she pulled out the envelope's contents and began to read. A few lines in, she got up and closed Terrell's office door.

The look on her face made Terrell sit up straight. "What is it, babe?"

"It's the answer to Ernest's earlier behavior, and questions about the center." She sat, shoulders squared, looking at Terrell. "He wanted to know where I'd be so he could serve me this motion seeking full custody of my son."

"Damn." Terrell sat back in his seat. "Well, at least now you know what's on his mind."

Chapter 24

A stunned Aliyah returned to work but left shortly afterward. She was too upset to focus on grams and milliliters, and such focus was too important when lives were at stake. Lauren had offered the distraction of a night at the theater. She'd passed on the show, knowing nothing short of a resolution would take her mind off of Ernest's special delivery. The invitation for Kyle to spend the night with Conner was gratefully accepted. Terrell had called twice. No, she didn't want company or to go out. Yes, she was doing okay. No, she hadn't been able to reach Ernest. Yes, she would call back later, and loved him, too.

She sat, in the afternoon quiet of her living room, turning over the day's events in her mind. Before the national exposure highlighting his intelligence, she couldn't have paid Ernest to visit Kyle and now he wanted full custody? He'd have a better chance of turning water to wine.

The ringing phone startled her out of her musings. After reading the ID, she snatched up her phone and tapped the speaker button. "Mom!"

"What's the matter, Aliyah? When listening to the message, you sounded upset."

"Upset is putting it mildly." For the first time since opening the envelope, tears flowed. In between sobs and expletives, she told her mom what had been going on. "Two months ago is when I heard from him, out of the blue. And because I want to handle this in a way best for Kyle, he's going to grow impatient and demand full custody? His son has waited five years to meet him. What should Kyle demand? That's what I want to ask him if he'll ever return my call."

"It doesn't surprise me that since he's famous and being touted as a little genius that they now want to claim him."

"Go ahead and say I told you so."

"Girl, I don't have to state the obvious. Nor is there any joy in being right all along. I've been around people like that before. When push comes to shove, they cling to their own kind. Now he wants to bring his son into the fold, and leave you with nothing."

"It'll never happen," Aliyah spat. "I'll do anything to keep my son with me. Anything."

"Well, I guess you need to start with a good lawyer. Do you know somebody who handles cases like this?"

"I'm going to call the same attorney who handled the case for child support. If he can't do it, hopefully he can recommend someone. Whatever happens, it has to be fast. The hearing is set for next month."

"So soon?"

"I know, shocked me, too. Knowing how they operate, strings were pulled to make it happen quickly, probably hoping that I won't have time to prepare a proper defense. But I'll be there, lawyer or no. Even if I have to walk in there armed with nothing but the power of my conviction, the truth of his absence and the strength of a mother's love, I'll fight. And I'll win."

"I believe you, baby. And your family will be supporting you every step of the way."

"I'm worried about you."

Three days had passed since Aliyah received the summons demanding that she appear in court regarding her son's custody. Terrell had tried to be supportive, and patient, but felt he was failing in both categories. Today, no matter what excuse she came up with to not come out, he wouldn't take no for an answer.

"I'm okay, Terrell. It's just taken a minute for the shock of Ernest's actions to wear off, and for me to mentally regroup and prepare for what's next."

"Which is?"

"Securing an attorney for the trial, which is happening this month."

"Whoa! How was the case able to get on a docket so quickly?"

"Westcott money, no doubt. I contacted the one who handled my paternity case, but he's not available. He's given my information to a colleague, but I have yet to hear from him. When I do, the first thing I'm going to suggest to the attorney is that we request a continuance for time to adequately prepare."

"Perhaps you should request his contact information and put in a call first thing Monday morning. Unless the judge grants the motion for a continuance, you have very little time to lose."

"I can't believe he's pulling this crap! Making it worse is the fact that this is not about Kyle. It's about prestige and control and image-building, and not having the world know that he has a son who forget about besides a small child support check has never take care of, but that he's never even met!"

"Baby, I can't imagine how upsetting this is for you, but try and calm down. The stress isn't productive."

"I know. I'm just so angry."

"And rightfully so. But you're doing everything that you're supposed to be doing. You've got to trust the process, and believe that justice will prevail."

"If justice doesn't, you can bet I will. I'll disappear,

take my son and leave the country. Change my identity and start a new life. Anything to make sure my son isn't taken away and subjected to a life with the Westcotts."

"Let's hope it doesn't come to that."

"Let's hope not. But if it does, I'll do it. I mean it. Protecting Kyle is all that's on my mind."

"I believe that, which is actually why I'm calling. Mom and Dad have made reservations at the club. Some type of announcement. I want you to come."

"Thanks, Terrell, but I'm not up to that kind of crowd right now."

"It's not going to be whatever type of crowd you're thinking. This is a private affair, like the dinner we had. Only family and a few close friends will be there."

"Oh, I still can't. Just remembered that Lauren and her family went out of town. Camping trip, I think."

"I considered that angle, which is why Betsy will be at our house taking care of the little ones. Kyle will get to have a play date with the twins. Next."

"Oh, don't sound so smug. I still don't want to go."

"I know you don't. But being consumed by this situation with Kyle's father isn't good for you. It's just a couple hours, babe. A chance to be distracted, if only for a little bit. Then later, I have some ideas for relieving the stress and tension from your body."

"Now that I can definitely use."

"I'm glad you're coming around. This isn't formal, but it is the club. Just put on something cute and sexy and be ready by six. I'm sending a car."

"That's not necessary."

"I know. But it's what's going to happen. I'll see you soon."

Aliyah was a woman of her word, but Terrell still breathed a sigh of relief when just after six his driver texted that he'd just picked her up and was on his way to the Paradise Cove Country Club. When she entered the private room thirty minutes later, his heart stirred. Not just because she looked stunning, which she did, in a deep red sheath-style dress with silver pumps and jewelry, but because just beyond the simple makeup, upswept do and polite smile Terrell detected the tenseness around her ruby-red mouth and the newly formed worry lines at the sides of her eyes. Worry lines that Kyle's father's callous actions had caused. In this moment Terrell realized two things. One, that he'd do anything in his power to take those signs of worry away. And two...he didn't like Kyle's father. Not at all.

He walked over to meet her. "You look beautiful, baby." They shared a hug. "How are you feeling?" His hands dropped to her shoulders. He lightly kneaded the tension.

"Better now."

He lowered his mouth to her ear. "Better still, later. I promise."

The sound of tinkling crystal got their attention. It was Jennifer, standing beside Ike, at the head of a long, rectangular table for twenty. Taking Aliyah's hand, Terrell led them to empty chairs near the front. Aliyah nodded hello when eye contact was made, and gave a subtle wave to Charlie and Warren, as she and Terrell sat across from them.

"Good evening, family. I'm sure you're wondering why we asked you here tonight for dinner. First of all I can allay any fears or concerns by saying that Jennifer and I are happier than we've ever been so there is no divorce on the horizon."

This caused a few titters. Everyone in the room knew that the Drakes had one of the strongest marriages on the west coast.

"And while this may be disappointing to some, I must also inform you that Jen is not pregnant."

A slight gasp and sharp punch to the arm was proof that even Jennifer was surprised at this comment. She joined everyone in laughter, though, and shook her head as she took a seat.

"Everyone here knows that although this is a family-owned business, no family members get a pass. In order to be a part of this company and most certainly to progress to higher levels within it, one must have the proper education, work ethic, natural ability and drive to go above and beyond the call of duty in their endeavors. Such is the case with the person whom I'd like to discuss tonight."

Terrell's brow creased. He looked at Ike, Jr., who shrugged. Others in the room showed similar confusion. Obviously very few if any besides Ike, Sr. knew the announcement that was about to come.

"Recently, something has been brought to the attention of one of our executives, which is leading to his unexpected and immediate departure from the firm. It's unfortunate, but necessary. This person has done exceptional work for many years. I consider him not only a valued employee, but a trusted friend. I'm speaking of Hugh Parker."

Terrell's confusion deepened. As VP of Sales, Hugh was his boss. And he was leaving? What had happened that would cause him to leave the company? And why hadn't Terrell been told about it?

Ike, Sr. smiled at Terrell. "I can see by the look on my son's face that he is as stunned as I was when Hugh came to me with the news that a family situation was causing him to have to relocate. In a moment, I'll let him share as little or much as he wants to about this personal issue but right now, I'd like to ask everyone to grab hold of your wine or champagne or shot glass, whatever you're imbibing, and help me congratulate and welcome Drake Realty's newest executive and Vice President of Sales, Terrell Drake."

Stunned didn't begin to convey how totally unexpected this news was to Terrell. For several seconds, he didn't move, waited for the cloud of confusion to lift. Only when he felt Aliyah's hand on his shoulder, and turned to see her smile and extend her glass, did he react to his father's announcement and the subsequent applause. He slowly rose from his seat and walked to where his dad stood. They shook hands and embraced. Proud father. Humbled son.

Aliyah took it all in, genuinely happy for Terrell's success. And glad she'd accepted his invitation. He'd been right. The break was needed. Tonight, she'd bask in the shadow of his happiness and the strength of his arms. Tomorrow would be enough time to renew her worries about Kyle, and the future.

Chapter 25

Sunday morning, after their standard pancake breakfast, Aliyah drove herself and Kyle to Sacramento and the movie theater where she and Terrell had agreed to meet. When she pulled into the parking lot, he was there waiting.

Aliyah got out. "Hey, Terrell."

"Hello."

She walked around to where Kyle was strapped into his booster seat and opened his door.

"Mr. Drake is here!"

"I see him, Kyle. Now unbuckle yourself and get out."

"Why is Mr. Drake here?" Terrell walked up next to Aliyah. "Mr. Drake, why are you here?"

"Let's go, boy."

"But, Mommy, I—"

"Do you want to see the movie or not?"

"Okay." Kyle blew out a breath as he unfastened the seat belt.

Aliyah looked at Terrell. "Did this child just huff at me?"

"No, not a huff. We teach them yoga at the center. I think he was practicing deep breathing."

"I can tell already. You're going to be no disciplinary help at all!"

Kyle's kiddie sneakers had barely met pavement before starting up again. "Mr. Drake. What are you doing here?"

"Well, I heard that a certain young man did very well

on a test recently. So I asked his mother, Aliyah, if I could come and help that young man celebrate."

"You're talking about me!"

"Oh, am I? Was it you who passed the test?"

"Yes," Kyle said, amid laughter. "You knew that."

They purchased tickets and after a stop by the concession stand for the obligatory box of popcorn, sweet treats and soda, the trio were happy to find seats together in the crowded theater. Aliyah sat between Terrell and Kyle. She got her son situated with his popcorn and candy, then turned to take the soda Terrell had been holding and placed it in the holder.

"I didn't expect an afternoon movie to be this crowded."

"That's because you don't have kids. This show will probably break box office records this weekend."

The movie was clearly aimed at the younger crowd, but while walking out, Terrell and Aliyah admitted they'd both liked it, too.

"What are we doing now?" Kyle asked Aliyah.

"If you're not too stuffed with popcorn, I thought we'd grab a bite to eat."

"Mr. Drake, will you come?"

Terrell looked at Aliyah. "If your mother doesn't mind."

"No, I don't mind."

"All right. Tell me where we're going and I'll meet you there."

The trip to Arden Fair Mall turned into a full afternoon and evening together. The decision to work off an all-American late lunch turned into a mini-shopping spree that included the Disney and Apple stores and one of Aliyah's favorites for Kyle, Abercrombie Kids. It also included her preventing Terrell from buying whatever she said she liked as a Christmas present. She'd never been overly materialistic and when dating Ernest, costly gifts usually ended up costing something extra. When she told Terrell she didn't want him to buy her anything, especially something extravagant, she meant it. By the time they headed to the parking garage, weariness had slowed Kyle's chatter to a minimum. A rare thing.

They stopped just inside the garage. "Where are you parked?" Terrell asked.

"Level two. What about you?"

"I'm down here. But I'll walk you to your car."

"Thanks but that's really not necessary. The elevators are right over here and our car is directly across from them."

"Are you sure?"

"Positive." Terrell followed as Aliyah headed to the bank of elevators.

"Call me when you head out. Let me know you're safe."

"Will do. Thanks for everything. Kyle, did you thank Mr. Drake for the gifts he bought you?"

"Yes, but I'll do it again. Thanks, Mr. Drake!"

"You're welcome, little man."

"I'm not little!"

Terrell took a step forward, towering over Kyle who though big for his age was no match for six-two. "You're littler than me."

Kyle looked respectfully sheepish and begrudgingly acknowledged this truth. "Okay."

On this funny note the three parted company. As promised, once on the freeway, Aliyah called Terrell.

"Just wanted to let you know we are on the freeway and headed home."

"How'd you beat me to the freeway and I was on the first floor?"

"I guess it comes with knowing how to drive."

"Whoa!"

"You forget I'm east coast. When it comes to knowing how to navigate we can teach you westerners a thing or two."

"Is that right?" Said as his voice dropped an octave.

"What do you think, Kyle?" Asked so that Terrell would know their call was not private.

"I can't drive so I don't know."

"Ha. Good answer. Terrell, we'll talk later, okay. Thanks again."

She disconnected the call and was about to turn up the stereo when Kyle spoke.

"Mom, can I ask you a question."

"Sure, babe."

"Do you like Mr. Drake?"

"Of course, Kyle. I try to like everybody."

"No, I mean *like him* like him. Like a boyfriend."

At this question, Aliyah was shocked but not surprised. She'd known this conversation was going to have to happen sooner or later. Tonight was as good a night as any. Still, she wasn't going to say more than necessary.

"I like him like a good friend. Mommy doesn't have a boyfriend."

"Do you want a boyfriend?"

"Maybe someday."

"I think Mr. Drake would make a good boyfriend."

"You do?" Kyle nodded. "Why is that?"

"Because he's nice. And smart. And rich, too!"

That last one was unexpected. "How do you know that?"

"'Cause I heard one of the teachers say that."

"Kyle, were you eavesdropping?"

"No, they were talking loud."

"Ha!"

"Mommy, if Mr. Drake was your boyfriend, would that make him my dad?"

Aliyah hesitated at Kyle's jump to this unexplored terrain, which was not only foreign, but stickier than the cinnamon bun Kyle had had for dessert.

"No. If Mommy were to date someone, that person does not become your father. If I were to ever get married, then that person may take on the role of your father. But you already have a daddy, Kyle, even though you've not met."

"Why not?"

"Because he lives far away, on the other side of the country, closer to Grandma."

"So."

Indeed. "So it's a long way to visit."

"But we visit Grandma. And Uncle Kieran came here."

"Yes, that is true." She took the opportunity while exiting the freeway to glance over at her son, gauge his expression. It was one of simple curiosity. About something that, in this moment, Aliyah understood he had every right to know.

"Would you like to meet your father?"

Kyle nodded. "I guess so."

"So if that were to happen, say in the next month or so, you'd feel okay about it?" Another nod. "I think it would be good for you to know your dad, so I'll see what I can do about that happening, okay?"

"Okay. But can I tell you something?"

"Sure?"

"If I could choose my own daddy, I'd choose Mr. Drake."

There was no comeback after a statement like that. So Aliyah didn't even try. She turned up the radio and joined Kyle in getting happy with singer Pharrell.

Chapter 26

"Are you ready for bright lights, big city, babe?"

"I'm more than ready!"

With December had come shorter days, cooler temps and just last night a dusting of snow. Aliyah had barely noticed, so focused had she been on the upcoming trial. Since their time in Sacramento, that and work had been her life. It had taken encouragement, begging and finally threats to pry her away from the computer and researching cases. She'd had several conversations with Mr. Simmons, the man her paternity attorney had recommended, the one who was preparing her custody case. They'd even had a "face-to-face" meeting via the internet. He'd told her not to worry, that the argument for her to maintain full custody was a strong one and that if for any reason the judge forced a joint arrangement, it should be gradual and at her convenience. Those words sounded nice but for all intents and purposes, Mr. Simmons was a stranger who, aside from his professional conviction, had zero attachment to the outcome of this case. This made Aliyah wary. She also met with Terrell's attorney friend, who'd been reassuring, but for Aliyah that wasn't enough. By the time they walked into that Rhode Island courthouse, she planned to be almost as well-versed in child custody law as he was. Meanwhile, this one-on-one adult time Terrell had planned was much needed.

They headed into the hangar. A familiar face was there to greet them. "Hello, Terrell. Aliyah."

"You remembered my name. Hi, Stan."

"I always remember a pretty lady," he said with a wink. "What's going on, big guy?"

"You got it, man," Terrell replied. They shook hands.

"So is it San Francisco again?"

"You didn't get my message?"

Stan pulled out his phone. "I guess not."

"I sent you some pertinent information. Check it out."

Terrell gave Stan a pat on the back as the three headed to the plane. Within minutes, they were airborne and headed east.

Once they got settled, Aliyah turned to Terrell. "What are we doing this time?"

"I didn't make plans for this trip. Thought we'd be spontaneous, just go with the flow."

"It must be nice to take off anytime you want, and do whatever it is you want to do."

"I don't look at my situation like that. I have responsibilities and obligations that don't allow for a leisurely lifestyle."

"I didn't mean to imply that yours was a life of leisure, but that when you do have the time, you also have the means to go where you want and do what you want. It's a lifestyle that most people don't even think about, let alone dream about."

"I guess you're right. When it's all you've ever known, you don't even think about it."

"That you had a privileged upbringing yet still treat the average person with decency is a testament to Jennifer and Ike and the way you were raised."

"My parents never let us think we were better, only blessed. As for decency," he said, pulling her closer to him and placing his hand on her inner thigh. "I want to change your mind about that by spending every moment in Sin City being as indecent as possible."

"Sin City?"

"Yes, we're headed to Vegas."

"How exciting!" She gave him a hug. "I've only been there once before. A weekend with a few of my classmates, to celebrate our graduation."

"It will only be for a weekend again. But we're going pack it full of fun."

He did exactly that. Packed not only with fun, but also with a sense of fantasy, too. Starting with their hotel suite, if one could call it that. Though it was at the top of the Palms Casino, to Aliyah, condo or apartment seemed more appropriate. One of seven luxury penthouses in this popular strip hotel, the suite was over three thousand square feet of pure luxury. From the floor-to-ceiling windows that offered some of the most amazing views in all of Vegas, to the gourmet kitchen, complete with on-call chef, to the 24-hour concierge and car service, everything was designed to make one feel special. Like royalty. Pampered. Loved.

After enjoying the stainless-steel pool table while playing with a special set of balls, Aliyah and Terrell showered and dressed for 7:00 p.m. dinner reservations at Ceasars Palace followed by front row seat at Mariah's show. It was a party crowd in the mood for a good time. Terrell and Aliyah joined right in, making friends with the couple next to them and once Mariah took the stage singing along with all of their favorites, and swaying to visions of love. The next day brought a helicopter ride to the Grand Canyon, dinner on a bluff and a night of making love in front of the two-way fireplace with the neon lights of the Vegas strip twinkling in the background. It was enough to make a woman lose her mind, fall in love and forget about any problem she'd ever had. Almost.

Sunday came and all too soon it was time to return to

California and reality. They arrived at McCarran International Airport and the terminal for private plane customers within minutes of the time Terrell had given Stan that they wanted to take off. One of several advantages Aliyah observed in taking a charter. No security line. No X-ray machine, removal of shoes or jackets. Just a smile, warm greeting from the pilot and on the plane you go.

When it came to the romance of their relationship, Terrell often made the first move. Not today. As soon as the plane had leveled, Aliyah unbuckled her belt and snuggled into his arms.

"This weekend was incredible. I needed it more than I realized."

Terrell placed an arm around her shoulders, gave one a light squeeze. "You're way more relaxed than when we left, that's for sure."

"Hard not to be, with a man who wanted to make love to me seven ways from Sunday."

"I didn't hear you complaining."

"Not at all."

"Good, because I'm not finished."

"Maybe not, but I have to go home as soon as we land. The situation with Ernest has had me distracted. I have a ton of studying to do and need to stay focused from now until we break for the Christmas holiday."

"That's cool." Without warning, Terrell lifted her out of the seat.

She yelped. "What are you doing?"

He situated her on his lap, with a leg on each side of him, then reached for his belt. "I'm getting ready to stroke that kitty," he murmured, underscoring the point by placing a hand beneath her dress and flicking her nub through her thong.

"Can we do that?" She looked behind her. "What if Stan comes out?"

"I guess we'll give him a show. Sit up for me, for a minute."

She did. He rose up enough to pull down his jeans and boxers. His ever-ready appendage bobbed a greeting. She looked first at his powerful manhood and then into his dreamy eyes. Once again he reached beneath the mini dress he'd seen at Ceasars Palace the night of the concert and returned to buy for her the next day.

"Did I tell you how much I like this dress?"

"Ooh." A gasp escaped from her mouth as he slipped a strong forefinger beneath the lace and ran it down the length of her folds—up, down, once, twice, a slide inside, wetness. And then...

Rip.

Aliyah's eyes, half-closed, flew open. "Terrell, you tore my panties."

"I did," he said, replacing his finger with his now rock-hard dick, sliding back and forth, becoming wet with her dew.

"Those were Victoria's Secret."

"I'll buy you some more."

Finding home, he lifted his hips. She lowered hers. He palmed her cheeks, softly squeezing as he slowly, completely filled her. Love-making, raw and hot, as if they hadn't done it once already before leaving the suite. Their passion grew as the plane descended, their mutual orgasm heightened by the surroundings, getting thoroughly sexed from forty thousand feet all the way down until the tops of houses came into view.

After catching their breath, Terrell kissed her quickly. "Come on, baby. Now that I've made you a member of the mile-high club, let's clean up real quick."

She scooted off his lap and stood. "Is that what that term means?"

"For some it is."

"Yes, those with private planes and private bathrooms."
Said as they both hurried through a spin-cycle shower.

"You'd be surprised. I know people who got initiated in
a regular plane, some while flying coach even."

"Eww. Please don't tell me that. It's hard enough for me
to sit in those seats as it is."

"Hey, to be forewarned is to be forearmed."

"That's disgusting."

"Yeah but sometimes nasty can be so nice."

Chapter 27

Over the next week or so, Terrell spent more time with Aliyah and Kyle. Family-oriented activities, even those involving little people, could actually be quite fun. Who knew? With as much time as he'd spent between PC and Davis, he'd seen very little this past week of his mom and dad.

Seconds after walking into the library, where his dad was enjoying a spot of brandy while his mother drank tea, he found out his absence hadn't gone unnoticed.

"Look, Ike! A stranger in our home?"

"See, I told you to start taking ginkgo biloba," Terrell replied, walking over to kiss his mother's forehead. "They say memory is one of the first things to go!"

"Bite your tongue, son!" Jennifer laughed. "You'd better hope you're in the shape I am by the time you're fifty-something."

"You know I'm teasing, Mom. You look as beautiful now as the day I was born."

"How much do you need, Terrell?" Ike, Sr. asked. "Pouring it on that thick means you must want something."

The jovial camaraderie continued as Terrell walked over and poured himself a brandy, before joining his mother on the leather couch that had been custom-made for the room.

"I do have something to share with all of you," Terrell said.

"You're getting married?"

"No, Mom."

"She's pregnant."

"Dad, really? Come on, now. You know I handle my business better than that."

"Taught by the best, you should."

"Oh, Lord," Jennifer gasped, in a feigned voice of desperation. "How much Drake can a poor woman take?"

"I got it, honest, Mom."

"That you did." She set her teacup in its saucer on the table. "What do you have to share?"

"I think it's time for your last bird to fly the coop. I'm ready to buy a home."

"Oh? What's brought this on?"

"I just think it's time." Said with a shrug. "I'm an executive now, almost thirty. Everybody else was almost out of the house by the time they were my age. Heck, Julian and London are out now."

"Because neither of your younger siblings live in the state. You have an entire wing to yourself, a private chef at your disposal, maid service and no mortgage. I know plenty of people who'd give their eyeteeth to be in your place."

"That's a mother talking, son. No matter how old you get they want to keep you tied to their apron strings. But I understand. The time comes in every man's life where they want to plant their feet on their own front porch."

"Just because I'm asking questions and offering opinions doesn't mean that I don't understand. This is about Aliyah, isn't it?"

"It's about me not wanting to be living in my parents' home when I turn thirty."

"Uh-huh. And it's about Aliyah not wanting to sleep with you in your parents' home even before then. You should have seen how embarrassed she was when I mentioned her being here."

"When'd you do that?"

"When she came out for Thanksgiving."

"Dang, Mom!"

She waved away his outburst. "Don't get all flummoxed over the matter. I wanted her to know that she was welcome here, as a grown-up. That she didn't have to sneak around or feel guilty. That, woman to woman, I understood. I think she appreciated it."

"I guess so. She didn't mention it."

"Good for her. A woman worth her salt will never tell a man everything."

Aliyah looked around her as she waited for the massive creation of gold-plated steel guarding Golden Gates to open and allow her medium-sized sedan to go through. Having been here a few times, she should have been used to the opulence of this, the most coveted section of not just Paradise Cove, but of Northern California. But she wasn't. The immaculately manicured lawns, marbled statues, colored fountains and more plant varieties than she could count never ceased to amaze her. Every time she came here was like entering wonderland.

Especially today. When Terrell called with the news that he wanted her opinion on some homes he'd be showing, she immediately played along. He'd often referred to the conversation from a month or so ago, when she called him up and flirted by pretending to be a potential buyer. She'd learned a thing or two about Mr. Terrell Drake during their whirlwind time together and figured showing her the room and decor wasn't the only thing he wanted to do during this walk-through. That's why there was nothing beneath her halter-styled maxi except sun-kissed skin.

Your destination is on the right. Upon hearing the GPS

instruction, Aliyah took one look at the understated yet undoubtedly overpriced home Terrell had selected to show her and burst out laughing. Even after she started working full-time and made six figures, she doubted she could afford any house located behind those dazzling golden gates. A doorknob, maybe.

Halfway up the walk, the door opened. Terrell stepped into the entryway. "You must be Ms. Robinson."

"I am."

He shook her hand and then pulled her into a kiss that began soft and easy, then turned ravenous.

She laughingly backed out of his embrace. "Gee, that is some way you have of greeting your clients, Mr. Drake."

"There's only one client I greet like that." He gave her lips another quick peck. "You look good. I like that dress."

"Thank you."

They went inside. The foyer was impressive, much smaller than the one in the Drake estate but made commanding by a modern-designed chandelier—wrought iron and crystal—that made for a stunning focal point. A short hallway led into the open-concept living, dining and family room with lots of windows and uninterrupted views.

"So…what do you think?"

"This. Is. Amazing."

"You like it?"

"It's one of the most beautiful homes I've ever seen." She stepped into the expansive living area, over to the fireplace and then to the windows. "I can't even imagine living in a home like this."

"Why not?"

"Have you seen the average New York apartment? One could probably fit in this living room, definitely the living and dining room combined. But there's so much space here. And the ceilings. I love that they're so tall."

"The two-story-high ceiling has been popular for a

while now. I love them also. They make the room appear even bigger than it is, and gives you a feeling of openness and freedom."

"Look at this kitchen!"

Terrell followed behind her. "Do you cook?"

"Not a lot, especially with my schedule. But with a kitchen like this I would, and definitely more often. This is beautiful. Look at these fixtures."

"Our designers are top-notch. We keep the look clean and neutral, so the owner can add their stamp."

"I don't know if I'd add anything."

"You wouldn't want to paint the walls or change the counters or back splash?"

"I don't think so. The ivory-colored walls add to the brightness, and these understated earth tones complement them perfectly."

"So if you were looking for a home, this is one you'd buy."

"With California's sky-high prices, I'd probably not see this home. My first would probably be a condo."

"Please send the technical doctor out of the room and bring in a woman who loves shopping and spending money when the sky is the limit."

"Okay. Put that way...yes. This is a home that would probably suit most women's tastes. So far, I can't think of anything I'd add or change."

"If you do, please let me know."

"Why? I'm not buying it."

"Right, but hearing your thoughts will help me prepare for possible buyer objections. And home designs in the future."

"Just as long as any assistance I provide is reflected in a proper commission."

"Consider it done." He reached for her hand. "Come on. There's more to see."

Chapter 28

Aliyah looked at the number and frowned. She recognized it; had seen it recently on Terrell's phone. But why was someone from the Drake estate calling her? She looked at Kyle, deep into a Disney movie, tapped the speaker button and closed her bedroom door.

"Hello?"

"Hello, Aliyah. It's Jennifer Drake."

"Mrs. Drake."

"Please, call me Jennifer. I hope you don't mind my calling. I asked Terrell for your number."

"No, not at all. I just can't imagine…is Terrell okay?"

"Terrell is fine, dear. I'm actually calling to speak with you."

"What about?"

"It sounded like a good idea in my head, but now, in the moment, I may be stepping way out of line."

Aliyah didn't like the sound of that at all. Had she heard about Terrell's intentions and was calling with a "steer clear" warning regarding her son. "If so, it wouldn't be the first time."

"Oh, my."

"No, not for you stepping out of line. I meant it wouldn't be the first time someone interfered in my…not interfered but—"

"Dear, interfering is exactly what I'm about to do and

if it makes you at all uncomfortable or you are not interested, just let me know and we'll both forget this call ever happened."

"Okay." But not really.

"It's about your upcoming court date. I hope you don't mind that Terrell shared just a bit of what's happening with your son, his father and his father's family. We Drakes are a very close-knit family. There is little if anything happening in our lives that isn't eventually known by all of us. So please don't be angry at him for discussing this with me. After our brief conversation concerning it, I pried him for details. I'm a very good prier."

Aliyah's laugh was genuine. She finally relaxed. A little. "I believe it."

"He told me about the status of your son's father's family, and the airs you endured while dating their son."

"That's a nice word to use for how I was treated."

"I'm sure there are others, but focusing on those is counterproductive and not why I called. I've heard of the Westcotts in Rhode Island."

"You have?"

"Yes, very indirectly. A dear friend of mine grew up on the east coast and is very connected to society there. Her family knows their family and, well, the circle tends to be one where most of us at least know of each other. What I'm saying is I can just about imagine what you've had to deal with, being considered common in their eyes. Not true of course. You're the polar opposite of that. But to those with superficial standards for judging. Because I know what you're up against, I'd like to offer a…consultation of sorts. You are headed into battle. I'd like to help ensure you're properly armored, starting with a tailored suit from my personal designer."

"Oh, Mrs. Drake, I couldn't—"

"You can, and you should. This fight is for something

most valuable. Your son. You should employ every available resource to make sure it's a fight you win."

A few days later, as Aliyah rode to family court in Providence, Rhode Island, along with her parents, her brother, Kieran, and Lauren to serve as a character witness, she was dressed in the tailor-made way Mrs. Drake had suggested, a conservative charcoal-colored pantsuit that fit perfectly and felt great. Paired with a matching designer handbag and pumps, along with a strand of classic pearls and matching post earrings, Aliyah knew the look was the type of classic, understated elegance that people like Mrs. Westcott would find properly impressive. At this moment, however, clothing was the last thing on Aliyah's mind. It was going to take more than designer clothes to win this battle. After what had transpired in the past forty-eight hours, it would take a miracle. She settled back in her seat, looking out at the overcast day as gray as her mood, the recent developments and the conversation about them she'd had last night with Terrell. Right before hanging up on him.

"Baby, calm down."

"Calm down? Don't tell me to calm down! Did you not hear what I just said? My attorney's got pneumonia, the judge has failed to grant a continuance and I've been assigned some court-appointed lawyer who knows me even less than Mr. Simmons who didn't know me at all!"

"I'm not saying you don't have every right to be upset. I want to help you, and that can happen more quickly if we're both rational and focused solely on winning. No matter who is representing you, no matter who is the judge, the only thing that matters is you having full custody of Kyle."

"Don't you think I know that? I'm more aware of that than anyone. What you're not aware of, what you don't know, is the Westcotts, and the type of power they wield in this state. And the judge is probably in the family's back pocket as well. It has made my chances of winning very unlikely, Terrell. So being calm, rational, any of that is just not going to happen right now. And if they try and take away my son, I'll act the kind of crazy that will make them think I invented the word."

They arrived at the courthouse. The court-appointed attorney met her in the lobby. Her family continued to the family division and the room where her case would be heard. For the next thirty minutes she conferred with the attorney. When she entered the courtroom she felt a little better about what was happening. But not much.

The room was smaller than she expected, looked nothing like those courtrooms seen on TV. Her eyes went straight to the Westcotts, sitting on the right side of the room, her family on the left. As if feeling her eyes on him, Ernest turned around. Seconds later, so did his mom. Aliyah took in Ernest's smug expression and his mother's judgmental face without flinching. But inside, she was a bundle of nerves wrapped in a blanket of trepidation.

Ernest whispered something to his mother, then stood and walked over. Aliyah straightened her shoulders, adopted a look of confidence she didn't feel and braced herself for what she hoped wouldn't become an ugly confrontation.

"Hello, Aliyah."

"Hi, Ernest."

"You look well. It's clear the California sun agrees with you."

I wish I could say the same about the Rhode Island winter. The thought popped up immediately. Fortunately, she squelched it before it escaped from her mouth.

"Thanks."

The right response even though she preferred the first one.

"Aliyah, I hope that after we've settled this matter, we can establish a civil relationship. For the sake of our son."

Said without actually choking on the phrase. If not for the nausea this comment caused, she might have been impressed. With Kyle in mind, however, she put her feelings about Ernest aside.

"I agree, and provided the judge acts with reason and I maintain sole custody, I'm prepared to act as civilly as I'm treated. I've talked to a therapist about our situation and she believes that if handled correctly, integrating your meeting Kyle and becoming a part of his life can happen with minimal disruption, either physically or mentally."

"I could have told you that, and thought I did. However, I'm glad that talking to a professional made you feel better."

"Ms. Robinson," her attorney called out. He motioned her to join him at the front table. Without another word, she left Ernest standing in the aisle.

"Ms. Robinson, I've just conferred with the Westcotts' attorney and they've presented a reasonable alternative to sole custody they'd like you to consider."

"The only consideration that is reasonable is for sole custody of my son to remain with me. Period. End of story."

"Look, I don't have to tell you about the Westcotts' influence. To have the case heard here when the child lives elsewhere is already a huge exception. The attorney they've hired is the best on the eastern seaboard. What they're willing to do is change the request to shared custody, fifty-fifty, between the two of you, provided you move here, to Rhode Island."

"You can't be serious."

"As the child's father I think it's reasonable—"

"Have you forgotten—" Remembering the size of the room and the stakes, Aliyah paused, took a breath and lowered her voice. "Have you forgotten that I'm in residency, in California? My suggestion is that Mr. Westcott consider a relocation. Why don't you share that and then tell me how he likes it."

He left to do her bidding, but Aliyah was done talking. Right now she figured her time would be better spent thinking about what countries didn't extradite and what could be her new last name. Because if the judge granted the Westcotts either joint or sole custody, Aliyah would take Kyle and go on the run. To get him, they'd have to find her first.

The door to the judge's chamber opened. He looked quite "judgely," Aliyah decided, like someone fair, with common sense. Then she saw him nod and smile at Mr. Westcott. Perhaps he was a fool.

Before she could decide, the door behind her opened. Whoever it was held no interest for her, until she took in the judge's scowl. She turned around. Her heart almost stopped.

Taking seats behind her family were Terrell, Julian and Jennifer. Another man, a bit older, attractive, dressed in a suit, said something to Jennifer before continuing forward. He smiled. She nodded and watched as the Westcott attorney and her court-appointed chap scurried forward to join the stranger as he approached the judge.

"Good afternoon, Judge."

"Afternoon, Counselor. Surprised to see you here. Your case is scheduled for next week."

"I'm ready for it, too, Judge. Which I can't say for the one I'm handling right now, that of Ms. Robinson and her son, Kyle. Having just been hired moments ago, I am going to need a bit of time, not much, to confer with my client. I request an immediate recess to do so."

She could tell the judge didn't like it. Or him. Aliyah couldn't be sure.

"This case is fairly straightforward. I'll grant you one hour."

"Thank you, Judge. Based on what I've learned so far, one hour is all I'll need."

The stranger walked over to a stunned Aliyah. "Ms. Robinson, if you'll come with me, please."

She did as requested, glancing at the Drakes as she passed by.

"Nice suit," Jennifer said.

Aliyah managed a smile, but didn't answer. Instead she spoke under her breath to the man beside her. "Who are you?"

"My name is Dave Butler. I've been hired by the Drakes to ensure you win your case. Which is good news for you. Because I don't lose."

Chapter 29

"I know I was there to witness it, but what just happened?"

Aliyah's father, Joe, who was staring out the window, turned and answered. "The Westcotts finally ran in to somebody with more money than them." His eyes then slid from the daughter he loved to the impressive young man now sitting beside her, the one who'd rarely left her side since court was adjourned not an hour ago.

They were all in Jennifer's suite at the Omni Hotel, where she'd suggested they meet to talk and regroup following the abrupt turn of events at the courthouse. Aliyah, whose relief from the stress of it all had caused a near swoon, sat at the end of a long couch, knees pulled to her chest, a pillow at her back and Terrell by her side. Joe, Aliyah's mother, Delores, and oldest brother, Kieran, sat at the dining room table. Terrell's brother, Julian, sat in one of two club-styled chairs, busily texting away on his phone. Jennifer, poised and totally unruffled, sat in the other. The attorney, Dave Butler, had just left.

Aliyah sat up. Placed her feet on the floor.

"Feeling better, Lee?"

Aliyah smiled at her mother. "A little."

"Do you need something to eat? Joe, go downstairs and see if they have a sandwich, or soup or something."

"Don't bother," Jennifer said, rising quickly. "I'll have room service bring something up."

"I'm not hungry," Aliyah said.

"I'll still place an order. At some point, we'll need to eat." Jennifer continued on into the bedroom.

Aliyah placed her chin in her hand, eyeing Terrell intently.

"What?"

"You never mentioned knowing an attorney here."

"That's because I didn't."

"How'd you find Attorney Butler?"

Terrence sat back, placed his right ankle over his left knee. "After talking to you yesterday, I was too distracted to work. Hearing you that upset really bothered me."

"I'm sorry. I didn't mean to—"

"Don't apologize. It's how you felt. I called Niko, told him what was happening over here."

"Who's Niko?" Delores asked.

"Terrell's brother," Aliyah answered. "And an attorney, also." She turned back to Terrell. "What did he say?"

"Nothing that could have helped you legally, of course, since his background is corporate law. But he remembered a former colleague who went to Brown. Got in touch with him, explained the situation. Then that friend knew somebody who knew somebody and the next thing I knew Niko was calling me with Dave Butler's phone number.

"Apparently Dave also grew up in Rhode Island, is very familiar with the Westcotts and also with the goings-on that happen during certain judicial processes. Most importantly, I hear that a few years ago he handled a case that involved a family of siblings in foster care being abused. Authorities had information about it but nothing was being done. At least not fast enough for Dave's liking. So he went to the media. You see how charismatic he is and how eloquent of a speaker. The cameras love him and I guess the media did, too. He beat a pretty loud drum and every time he did, it got coverage. Things happened quickly after that and those children were saved from a very dire future. Looks like he's been somewhat of a media darling ever since.

"There's probably more to the story than any of us will ever know, but the about-face that the judge did in granting a continuance leads me to believe that something shady was happening in that courtroom and if he hadn't gotten his way, Dave Butler was about to go to the press and turn on a big old spotlight."

"What you've just told us is story enough. For the West-cotts, appearances, status and perception are everything. The very last thing in life they'd want is negative publicity." A slow smile spread across Aliyah's face. "That's it! Why didn't I think of this before?"

"What?" It was the first word Kieran, who adored his sister and hated to see her sad, had spoken since they arrived.

"The next time I talk to Ernest, I'll let him know that if he continues to seek full custody of Kyle, I'll go straight to *TMZ*."

Kieran shook his head. "That fool probably won't know what that is."

"You're right, and as angry as I am, and as much as he deserves it, I would never stoop so low as to do something like that."

"All's fair in love and child custody cases. Except my choice would be the *Providence Journal*." This suggestion from Julian, with eyes still glued to his phone.

"The local newspaper?" Terrell asked.

"Yes. Not too long ago, they did a story on Dave."

"My attorney?"

Julian nodded.

"That's what you've been doing, reconnaissance on Dave Butler?"

"Gathering information is what the internet's for."

Jennifer walked out of the bedroom. "Soup, salad and sandwiches are on the way. I hope someone's hungry."

"I'm glad you went ahead and ordered, Jennifer." Aliyah released a sigh as she stretched. "I'm feeling a little hungry after all."

Aliyah's optimistic mood lasted for another hour. Until she received a text from Ernest, requesting a meeting. She agreed to meet him, knew that as little as she looked forward to this conversation it was one that had to happen. At Terrell's insistence, she suggested they meet in lobby. "In case you need backup," he explained.

Turns out, neither back up nor threats was needed. When Ernest met her, it was to let her know that in re-thinking the situation regarding the development of his relationship with Kyle, he now felt it best to proceed at a more conservative pace. That once they'd known each other a while, and Kyle was a little older, the custody arrangement could be revisited.

Aliyah listened and agreed. No need to expound on her definition of "a little older," even though Kyle would be eighteen and grown before she relinquished custody. But the meeting had gone so much better than she had expected, she figured this tidbit counterproductive. Ernest and the rest of his family would find out soon enough.

A week before Christmas, Ernest flew to Sacramento to spend time with the son he'd not seen. The interaction was initially awkward—Ernest obviously not used to being around children, Kyle overwhelmed and shy in the company of "Dad." Kyle got a mountain of early Christmas gifts and Ernest took pictures, no doubt to use in his new claim to fame. Aliyah didn't too much begrudge this. Who wouldn't want to be known as her son's father? Kyle was amazing! Still, when they stood to part ways at the restaurant, she could have sworn that the look on Ernest's face was one of relief.

On the way home, Aliyah quizzed Kyle. "Did you enjoy the visit, Kyle, spending time with your father?"

"It was okay, I guess. He talks kind of funny. But I liked his watch. It was like a computer! But he doesn't know how to play video games. Mr. Drake can play way better than him. Ernest is my father, but I think Mr. Drake is way cooler."

Aliyah looked at her son and smiled. "You know what, buddy? I think so, too."

Chapter 30

Filled with work and Ernest's visit to meet Kyle, the days passed in a blur. It was Christmas Eve, and neither Terrell nor Aliyah had to work until after the New Year. Both were grateful for the break. The excitement in the air came not only from the opportunity to relax and enjoy each other, but also because Aliyah would be enjoying her family as well. The drama in Rhode Island had brought the families closer. Julian and Kieran were becoming fast friends. Her family initially balked at the generous invitation, but after much cajoling and a little bribery, the Robinsons had accepted the Drakes' invitation to spend the holiday in Paradise Cove.

Terrell arranged a limo to be sent to the airport but in the end, Aliyah was too excited to wait the forty-five minutes to an hour it would take for them to get from San Francisco. She and Terrell ended up riding along.

They met them at baggage claim, then walked to the car. When she reached the limo, her father stopped in his tracks. "Is this for us?"

"Yes, Dad. It was either this or a van to get all of us in one vehicle."

"You picked us up in style," he murmured, shaking his head as he climbed inside the designer stretch. "The last time I rode in one of these it was for a funeral. I was about to ask you who died."

It took a minute and some maneuvering but soon all of the luggage and all of the Robinsons were in the limo and headed to Paradise Cove. It was the first time on the west coast for all except Aliyah's father, who'd visited LA in his twenties, and Kieran, who'd helped his sister move. Delores was unusually animated as she remarked on the wide-open space and coastal beauty. Having spent most of her life surrounded by brownstones and skyscrapers, her mother said she felt like traipsing through the fields they passed like Julie Andrews did in *The Sound of Music*. The miles flew by quickly as Terrell answered questions and provided a running commentary of the area he'd lived in his entire life.

They reached Paradise Cove. "This town is so pretty," Delores exclaimed. "And so clean!"

Joe whistled. "We're not in Prospect Heights, that's for sure."

As they neared Golden Gates, Aliyah turned so that she could surreptitiously watch her parents' reaction. When the limo stopped and the gates began to open, their expressions did not disappoint.

"You live here?" Her sister Danaya asked, eyes filled with wonder as she looked around.

Aliyah laughed. "I wish. The Drakes are in real estate. There is a vacant property that has yet to sell. So instead of putting you up in a hotel, he offered to let you guys stay there."

Minutes later, the limo pulled into the driveway of a Tuscany-styled home. Its tan exterior, rich mahogany-colored roofing and deep red shutters and front door stood out among the other homes with subtler features.

"This is it?" wide-eyed Danaya asked Aliyah.

"Yes, this is home sweet home."

"Wow." Danaya pulled out her cell phone and began to take pictures. "I'm in Hollywood!"

"How big is this place?" Joe asked. The question was asked casually, but knowing her dad she figured he was counting Drake money.

"Huge," Aliyah answered. "You'll see."

They entered the fully furnished home. "I thought you said nobody lived here," Delores said, looking around at the elegant furnishings.

"No one does. All of this—" she began with a wide sweep of her hand "—is called staging. The homes are furnished to give potential buyers a homey feel, and make it easy to imagine themselves in it."

"I can't imagine living in a home as nice is this," Delores admitted.

"Me, either," Aliyah replied.

"I can," Danaya sang, dancing to music that only she heard. "Lee, which room do I get?"

"There are five bedrooms so you have choices. Let's go pick one out."

"I want the master suite!"

"Keep wanting!" Delores called out. "I might not see myself living here, but I'm sure going to enjoy spending the night."

After getting everyone settled into the show home, the limo took them all over to the Drake estate. The Robinsons had thought Terrell's home impressive but upon seeing where his parents lived, their jaws dropped. Aliyah watched her parents grow pensive as they walked to the entryway. However, any discomfort they may have felt disappeared with the sincerity of Jennifer's warm embrace, and Ike Sr.'s inviting Joe for a spot of brandy.

After introducing her parents to Ike, Sr., she continued with her siblings. "This is the next oldest, my brother, Kieran, my brother Joseph, Jr., who we all call JoJo, my brother Myles, and my youngest sister, Danaya. Guys, this is Mr. Drake."

"Please," Jennifer said while reaching to embrace Kieran in a light hug. "Just Jennifer and Ike is fine. My family is out back, waiting to meet all of you. Right this way, please."

Gathered around the pool in the backyard were Niko, Monique, Ike Jr., Warren, Charlie, Teresa, Atka, Julian and London. The only one of Ike and Jennifer's children not present was Reginald who, after spending Christmas with his wife's family, would fly out for New Year's Eve. On a nearby table was a casual spread of barbecued meats, root veggies and salad that would be washed down with ice-cold lemonade or chilled wine. When the Drake men found out Kieran was a basketball star in Iowa, trash talking abounded. They'd barely wiped the last bit of sauce from their fingers before heading to the courts for some basketball bonding. Those who stayed behind enjoyed a glass of vintage wine from the Drake cousin's vineyard, and a mildly chilly evening conversing around the outdoor fireplace. By the time the men returned from the basketball court Aliyah's parents were tipsy, she and Terrell were tired and everyone was ready for bed and looking forward to the next day.

Christmas morning arrived warm and sunny. Used to cooking a large meal for both hers and the extended family, Delores hardly knew how to simply relax and wait for a catered meal. But when Jennifer suggested they all get manicures, pedicures and facials from an in-home spa company that worked on holidays, Delores happily agreed. She later told Aliyah that Jennifer's lifestyle was one she could get used to. Aliyah's heart warmed. Nothing would make her happier than for her family to move out west. With her dad a die-hard New Yorker, that would indeed be a miracle move.

They took separate cars—Aliyah's parents with Ike, Sr. and Jennifer; Kieran with Niko and Monique, JoJo, Myles, Danaya and Kyle with Terrell and Aliyah—and the rest in cars of their own. For the Robinsons the surprises continued when the sophistication of the homes in Golden Gates gave way to the casual yet chic comfort of Warren's ranch. The families enjoyed a veritable feast of turkey, ham and freshwater salmon from the Drake Lake project, with all of the usual holiday trimmings rounding out the menu. Several friends and extended family members joined them, including Lauren and her crew, Luther and his family and others from the realty company, the ranch and the center, who'd found themselves away from their own families on this special day.

Shortly after dinner was over, as most were relaxing in and around the pool in Warren's backyard, their conversation was interrupted by the loud sound of a low-flying plane heading in their direction.

Teresa shielded her eyes from the sun and leaned toward her husband. "That plane is quite low, honey, don't you think?"

Atka nodded. "Yes, unless it's landing somewhere nearby."

"Has a landing strip been built out here?" Ike, Jr. inquired.

"Not that I know of," Warren replied.

"Looks like there's a sign or something trailing behind it." At Julian's observation, everyone looked up.

"Oh, one of those message planes," Jennifer said.

"I wonder who it's for."

Terrell, who was standing directly behind Aliyah, wrapped his arms around her and answered, "I have no idea."

Everyone was quiet, waiting for the message to come into view. As it did, Aliyah read it out loud:

"Will...you...marry...me..." As the plane reached them, a banner dropped from the window, completing the question. "Aliyah?"

For a beat, nobody moved. Then everyone reacted at once.

"Oh, my God!"

"That's cool!"

"It says Aliyah!"

"Mommy! That's your name!"

Aliyah turned to Terrell, who wore a smug, satisfied grin. "Terrell, what is this?" Her eyes glittered with unshed tears.

"Part of your Christmas present. Since you'd never tell me what you wanted, I had to improvise." He pulled out a blue box and got on one knee. "Will you do me the pleasure of becoming Mrs. Drake?"

"Yes!" Aliyah threw her arms around him as everyone cheered.

"Where are we going?"

After being surrounded by thirty people for a weekend, and with Kyle at his second home, the Hensleys, Aliyah was looking forward to spending a quiet New Year's Eve at her humble abode.

"I need to go check on a property real quick."

"Now? Tonight?"

"Yes, where your family stayed. It will only take a minute. I'll be showing it next week and just want to make sure the cleaning company did their job."

"Oh, okay." They reached the home that Aliyah's family had fallen in love with. "Make it quick."

"For that to happen, you'd better come with me."

"Terrell, just hurry up."

"Come on! This client I'm working with is as finicky

as they come. I need a woman's eye to make sure everything is in the right place."

Her compliance was preceded by a harrumph and a sigh, but Aliyah got out of the car and followed Terrell up the stairs. He opened the door, then stood back to let her enter.

"You had this done so quickly, Tee. The family just left today." All except Kieran, who'd decided to hang out with Julian, who'd encouraged him to move here. "That was quick."

She continued into the living room, noticed the fireplace mantel and stopped short. "What are my family's pictures doing here?" Slowly, she moved forward, stopping in front of one of her favorite pictures of her parents. It had been taken when they were her age.

"And here's me! Where'd you get…when did you do this?"

Terrell feigned ignorance. "Those weren't there before?" She swatted his arm. "Maybe your mother put them to, you know, make the place more comfortable, to feel more like home."

"You may be right. And in the rush to get to the airport, probably forgot them." She went back to the pictures. "Well, too bad, because she won't get them back now. I'm taking them home with…"

Her words slowly faded away as she reached for the card propped up behind the pictures:

Ms. Robinson: Thank you for helping me close the deal. The house is yours. Welcome home.

"This isn't."
He nodded. "It is."
"All that time you told me about a finicky buyer?"
"You can be kind of finicky."
That statement produced a jaw drop. "I am not finicky."

"And a bit stubborn, too."

"I can't believe you tricked me. Or are you tricking me now?"

"No trickery," he replied, closing the distance between them. "Later, you can ask your mom. She helped me with the pictures."

"Mom knew, too?!"

"Not until a couple days ago. I swore her to secrecy."

"Look at you. Barely in the family and plotting against me."

"I've got it like that, babe. I thought that's why you loved me."

Later, Terrell walked from the kitchen with two drinks and joined Aliyah, who was lounging in in a faux mink, upscale, oversized beanbag by the burning fireplace. He'd teased her when she'd seen it in a vintage shop and fell in love. Now it was one of their favorite places to cuddle.

"This holiday was crazy fun!" He handed her the glass.

"Thank you, babe." She took a sip. "It's hands down the best Christmas season I've ever had. I've never seen my family so happy. Mama is ready to move out here and even Daddy had to admit that the idea of never having to shovel snow again was appealing. I still can't believe JoJo at your parents' house, teaching Kyle how to slide down the banister."

"You forget that at one time that place housed six knuckleheads, a tomboy sister and an irksome diva. There isn't a thing your brothers could have done that we haven't done or at least tried."

"Thank you for that."

"For what?"

"Treating my family so kindly; making them feel welcome. All of your family was wonderful."

"You're welcome, but it was my parents who issued the invitation. Specifically, my mom."

"I know and I thanked her, too. But I saw how you went out of your way to include them, especially my dad. He's a simple guy, used to the ordinary and at times felt uncomfortable, almost overwhelmed. You saw that and made sure he wasn't left out of whatever was happening. I saw Warren doing that, too."

"Anyone who's important to you is important to me. And anyone who's important to me, is important to my family. That's Drake, baby. That's how we roll."

She nestled deeper into his arms. They shared a quick kiss. "This holiday season was so wonderful it felt unreal. A part of me is like, wow, did that really happen?"

"It certainly did. In fact, I think somebody got engaged."

"Someone most certainly did." She held out her hand, watched the fire and the subdued lighting make the three-carat diamond sparkle and flash. "I keep thinking someone will pinch me and I'll find out I'm dreaming. Ouch!"

He chuckled. "I couldn't resist it, baby. You've got so much goodness back there to pinch."

"There are no words to describe how beautiful this ring is, babe. I won't be able to wear it often, but when I do, it will be with such pride."

"What do you mean? You can't take off your wedding ring."

"Of course I can."

"Why?"

"During cleaning, for one, or washing dishes. Would you like it to accidently slip down the drain while I'm rinsing a glass or flatware? And then there's work. I think it's too flashy for a hospital setting."

"Married male doctors don't wear wedding bands?"

"Not with large diamonds that can double as an assault weapon."

Terrell laughed. "I guess I see your point."

"I'll wear the band," she said, running her hand beneath his sweater to run her nails down his chest. "Even if wearing nothing at all, I'll be your wife regardless."

"Good to know, since that will be your state of dress most of the time."

"That might prove a bit traumatic for Kyle."

"Ha! Correction, in the master suite."

"That could possibly be arranged. And speaking of arrangements, we need to talk about your desire for me and Kyle to move in with you ASAP."

"What, are you going to tell me we have to be married first?"

"No, though that would be nice. But there's more to consider."

"Like what?"

"Like Kyle transferring schools in the middle of the year, and my no longer having Lauren and her family right around the corner to help me take care of him, and they help me a lot. Not to mention my residency at UC Davis and interning at Living Medical, that continues for at least another year and a half. I know it's not a long commute but moving here there are a variety of logistics that would have to be worked out."

"None of that is a big deal," Terrell replied, dismissing her concerns with a wave of his hand. "That's what help and assistants and nannies are for. So first of all, if you think it will be too disruptive, then Kyle can stay where he is until summer. You'd still do the residency at UC, of course, but construction is almost complete on the PC's urgent care center. Not sure what kind of staff it takes to run it. But maybe you could do your interning there."

"Possibly, but that still doesn't solve the problem of Kyle being cared for or my commute."

"A live-in nanny, someone he knows, like Miss Marva, who sometimes watched me when I was young. We can also hire a driver so that you can study or read or do whatever you need to make your commute time beneficial, or sleep at the end of those long, hard shifts. Next excuse, I mean, problem, Ms. Robinson?"

"You know what? Your brother's nicknamed you correctly, Silky."

"No! Not you, too!" Terrell said, while jokingly pushing her away. "They used to drive me crazy with that nonsense, all because of my skills when it came to the ladies."

"Oh, really? What skills are those?"

He slid his eyes over her with a look of supreme confidence. "All of the ones that have you about to become Mrs. Drake. Uh-huh, now. Those skills, baby."

She swatted him. "Shut up, you're so cocky. Mr. Silky, smooth-as-silk," she added, mimicking his brothers. "And before you can say it, yes, Terrell Drake, that's what I love about you."

* * * * *

Everyone in the room turned at the same time.
Gianna Martelli stood in the doorway, a bright smile
painting her expression. Donovan pushed himself up
from his seat, a wave of anxiety washing over him.
Gianna met his stare, a nervous twitch pulsing at the edge
of her lip. Light danced in her eyes as her gaze shifted
from the top of his head to the floor beneath his feet and
back, finally setting on his face.

Donovan Boudreaux was neatly attired, wearing a
casual summer suit in tan-colored linen with a white dress
shirt open at the collar. Brown leather loafers completed
his look. His dark hair was cropped low and close, and
he sported just the faintest hint of a goatee. His features
were chiseled, and at first glance she could have easily
mistaken him for a high fashion model. Nothing about

him screamed teacher. The man was drop-dead gorgeous, and as she stared, he took her breath away.

The moment was suddenly surreal, as though everything was moving in slow motion. As she glided to his side, Donovan was awed by the sheer magnitude of the moment, feeling as if he was lost somewhere deep in the sweetest dream. And then she touched him, her slender arms reaching around to give him a warm hug.

"It's nice to finally meet you," Gianna said softly. "Welcome to Italy."

Donovan's smile spread full across his face, his gaze dancing over her features. Although she and her sister were identical, he would have easily proclaimed Gianna the most beautiful woman he'd ever laid eyes on. The photo on the dust jacket of her books didn't begin to do her justice. Her complexion was dark honey, a sun-kissed glow emanating from unblemished skin. Her eyes were large saucers, blue-black in color, and reminded him of vast expanses of black ice. Her features were delicate, a button nose and thin lips framed by lush, thick waves of jet-black hair that fell to midwaist on a petite frame. She was tiny, almost fragile, but carried herself as though she stood inches taller. She wore a floral-print, ankle-length skirt and a simple white shirt that stopped just below her full bustline, exposing a washboard stomach. Gianna Martelli was stunning!

Don't miss
TUSCAN HEAT by Deborah Fletcher Mello,
available January 2016 wherever
Harlequin® Kimani Romance™
books and ebooks are sold.

*Opposites attract...
and ignite!*

PHYLLIS
BOURNE

*Heated
Moments*

When she's dumped as the face of Espresso Cosmetics, Lola Gray
hits the road. When a speeding ticket gets her in trouble in a small
town in Ohio, the only bright spot is the hunky local police chief.
Dylan Cooper relishes the peace and quiet of Cooper's Place. Now
the stunning tabloid beauty he is holding for questioning is charming
his hometown and seducing him. Will their sizzling affair become a
lifetime of love?

ESPRESSO EMPIRE

Available December 2015!

HARLEQUIN®
www.Harlequin.com

KPPB431215